Alive and Well in Prague, New York

Alive and Well in Prague, New York

Daphne Grab

LAURA GERINGER BOOKS
HARPER
TEEN
An Imprint of HarperCollins*Publishers*

HarperTeen is an imprint of HarperCollins Publishers.

Alive and Well in Prague, New York
Copyright © 2008 by Daphne Benedis-Grab
For information address HarperCollins Children's Books,
a division of HarperCollins Publishers,
1350 Avenue of the Americas, New York, NY 10019.
www.harperteen.com

Library of Congress Cataloging-in-Publication Data
Grab, Daphne.
Alive and well in Prague, New York / by Daphne Grab. — 1st ed.
    p.   cm.
"HarperTeen."
Summary: Manhattanites Matisse Osgood and her artist parents
move to upstate New York when her father's Parkinson's disease
worsens, and Matisse must face high school in a small, provincial
town as she tries to avoid thinking about her father's future.
  ISBN 978-0-06-125670-7 (trade bdg.)
  ISBN 978-0-06-125671-4 (lib. bdg.)
  [1. Parkinson's disease—Fiction. 2. Fathers and daughters—Fiction.
3. Family life—New York (State)—Fiction. 4. High schools—Fiction.
5. Schools—Fiction. 6. Country life—New York (State)—Fiction.
7. New York (State)—Fiction.] I. Title.
PZ7.G7484Al 2008   2007018676
[Fic]—dc22   CIP
                                                                    AC

Typography by Carla Weise
1 2 3 4 5 6 7 8 9 10
❖
First Edition

For Greg

Chapter One

"Okay, honey, this is it!" My mother's voice rang with false cheer, too loud inside the little Honda she was still figuring out how to drive. She hit the brakes and the car slid slightly on the wet pavement.

I grabbed at the door for safety but accidentally opened it. Rain sprayed in, splashing on my dress.

"Damn," I muttered, slamming the door. I wasn't used to being a passenger any more than she was used to driving. "Even the weather here sucks."

"It did rain back home, too, sweetie," she

said. Her hands played absently with the silk scarf looped around her neck. She plucked at one of the splatters of paint that stuck to its fringe. "I know the first day is hard, but I'm sure you'll make friends fast."

I pulled a napkin out of the glove box and began blotting my dress. "I can't even say the name of the stupid school." I glanced out the window, through the gloomy wet, to the blue letters on top of the ugly brick building: Miloslsv High.

"I'm sure there's a great story about how the school got such an unusual name," she said.

I snorted.

"Seriously, honey! I bet you'll come home laughing about it."

"Yeah, that's what's gonna happen," I muttered. I crumpled the napkin and put it back in the glove compartment.

"Matisse, small-town living might surprise you. There really is a lot happening here."

"What, is there a gallery opening I missed in the *Prague Post*?"

"Well, it's what Dad needs right now," she

said. I looked down at the water stains on my dress as silence filled the car. I willed my mom not to make this morning worse by reminding me of the real reason we'd moved here. I didn't need to think about that before my first day at the lamest high school in existence.

"You know—" she started.

I grabbed the messenger bag at my feet and snatched the black umbrella lying next to it. "I'm out of here," I said, opening the door and trying to push open the umbrella to protect myself from the downpour. I succeeded only in poking my cheek and spraying water into the car. "I'll walk home," I said as I shut the door.

Her "'Bye, sweetie" was muffled by the rain pelting down around me.

I took baby steps up the path toward the main entrance, trying to keep my shoes dry. For the millionth time I considered the terrible irony of moving to Prague, a town named after one of the coolest cities in the world, yet pretty much the most pathetic place I'd been to in my entire life. I still couldn't believe my parents had chosen to leave our home in New York City to live here. We'd been in Prague three weeks and I still kept expecting to wake up in our condo on West Seventy-Eighth Street, with the best movies, restaurants, museums, and galleries a short subway ride away. Instead I woke up to the thrilling possibility of seeing one of the two second-run movies playing in town or eating at the local pizza place, where they didn't even have sun-dried tomatoes as a topping. And the nearest museums and galleries were back home in New York City, about four hours away. It was like moving from downtown paradise to the suburbs of hell.

Once I got inside the cramped school lobby, I shook out my umbrella. The walls were a pukey shade of green, and the dim fluorescent lights made me feel like I was stuck in a warehouse. My old school, Upper West Side Friends, was in a gorgeous brownstone, with a big fireplace in the lobby and couches where we hung out before school. You know things are bad when you long for a school lobby.

Around me girls shrieked and guys slapped one another on the back. People glanced at me

 4

as I strode past. I heard a girl mutter, "Nice dress," and then laugh with her little group of friends. My black vintage Jackie O style *was* nice; much too nice to be appreciated in this dump.

I turned a corner and was practically trampled by a hefty blond hick wearing overalls. He looked like he belonged in a performance of *Oklahoma!*

"Sorry! Hi there," he called, as he clomped past me, his thick hair sticking out absurdly.

I made a wrong turn but finally managed to find my locker. A girl next to me with perfectly curled hair was standing in front of her open locker. I noticed she was taping up pictures of girls with their arms around one another and guys in football gear. She secured the last one, slammed her locker shut, and then caught sight of me.

"Hello there," she chirped, bouncing slightly on her toes. "You're the new girl. We haven't had one of those in a while. I'm Sherry. Welcome!"

She paused, then skipped off down the hall,

leaving a cloud of perfume behind.

I sighed as I set my stuff inside my tiny puke-green locker. It was going to be a long day.

• • •

Sure enough, by sixth period I felt like I'd been locked in Miloswhatever High for half my life. I dragged myself into the art room and sat at the only empty table, a flimsy, paint-splattered contraption that teetered when I put my bag on it.

The teacher was a plump woman with frizzy curls. She hugged a few kids before walking to the desk to call roll, another quaint tradition we didn't have at Friends. When she got to my name, instead of tripping over it like my other teachers today had, she looked up and gave me a big smile.

"Matisse, what a beautiful name! Did you know there's a famous artist with that name?"

Obviously I knew that—I was named after him! And if she'd had any shred of art knowledge, she would've been more impressed by my last name. Osgood was a name that sent art lovers across the world into a frenzy. But it blew right past this woman, who was still smiling at me.

"He paints beautiful lily pads and haystacks," she said.

I was floored. Monet painted that stuff, not Matisse.

"Yes, I've been to Giverny twice," I said, giving her a chance to correct her mistake.

Her forehead wrinkled.

"Well, I'm not sure where Jeevernee is," she said finally, badly mispronouncing the name of Monet's home and famous gardens outside Paris.

I hadn't cried, not a single tear in over two years, but an art teacher who didn't know the difference between Monet and Matisse brought me awfully close.

After school I walked into town. The rain had stopped, and I wanted to get a new book on my way home. Two girls brushed past me on the sidewalk, their heads bent together. For a second I thought of the first day of school last year, Ceese and I walking uptown to the Mocha Bean while she told me all about meeting James in drama class. Of course, all that had changed, but walking with Ceese on the first day of school—that was a good day.

It was only a few blocks from the high school to the main street of Prague. There were a couple of stores, a sad little park with a run-down playground, and a parking lot with five or six cars in it.

I walked up to the bookstore, and as I reached for the door, three kids pushed their way out. Two guys—who looked like twins in their jeans and football jerseys—came first, followed by a girl in a bright pink minidress. They were so intent on their conversation that they didn't even notice when they hit me with the door.

"Man, what was *with* that guy?" the girl asked.

"What a freak!" one of the guys with her said. The other guy started jerking and shaking his arms. They all cracked up.

"That's just how he looked!" the girl crowed.

I froze, unable to tear my eyes away from the guy waving his arms. He had added grunting sounds to his act, and the girl was doubling over. The blood in my veins turned to ice, sweat pricked my temples, and my breath was stuck, pressed down tight in my chest. I couldn't move or think—not that I had to. I knew the freak they were making fun of.

I didn't need to go inside to see it was my father.

Chapter Two

Six years ago my father was injured when he fell off a ladder. He was working on a sculpture that the city had commissioned him to do in Carl Schurz Park. He hit his head on the base of the sculpture and knocked himself out. The doctor told him he was lucky to have only a concussion but to keep an eye out for lingering problems. When my father's left hand started to shake a few months later, he chalked it up to the accident, figuring it wasn't a big deal and that it would go away on its own. But two months later it was still shaking. My mom finally forced him back to the doctor, who sent him to a neurologist.

About a thousand tests later the whole family was called in to hear his diagnosis: Parkinson's disease, or PD, as the neurologist affectionately called it.

"It's a lot better than it sounds," the doctor said as I fought not to throw up. My mom gripped her purse so hard, her knuckles turned white. "We have some great meds—they can suppress the symptoms for years."

PD is a neurological disease that involves the death of certain nerves in the brain. This leads to loss of muscle control, meaning that it was going to be harder and harder for my dad to be in charge of his own body. The symptoms get worse over time.

"It's not something to panic about," the doctor said, in what he apparently thought was a soothing voice. "The disease may progress very slowly; we just don't know at this point."

"It *may* progress slowly?" my dad said.

"It's difficult to predict," the doctor said. "We just have to wait and see. You could live with the disease for a very long time."

That was the moment I stopped wanting to

hear or even think about PD.

"He gives it a nickname because he's making millions off it," my dad muttered as our family walked out of the office, sick with shock over the news. He stormed off to the drugstore to fill the prescriptions the doctor had given him.

"Don't worry, honey," my mom said to me, her voice high and tight. "The doctor said it was probably at the beginning stages, so he won't have bad symptoms or anything for a while."

But the doctor, who my dad sarcastically dubbed "the Genius," ended up being wrong. The drugs, which subdued all my dad's symptoms at first, became less effective after only three years, leaving him with longer "off" periods when the symptoms could not be masked. He moved slowly, which made things like getting dressed take ages; he had tremors; and at times his arms and legs got so rigid that he couldn't move them. His face, once always relaxed and animated, became stiffer, and even during an "on" period it never looked like it used to. For longer and longer blocks of time, my dad was subservient to the disease; PD had taken over.

It was last year, after the Genius told my dad

that he couldn't work on large sculptures anymore, that things got really bad. You could see the doctor's point: my dad up on a ladder, handling a blowtorch and lots of toxic chemicals, not being able to react quickly if something went wrong. But for my dad it was the worst thing that had ever happened to him. He'd been a sculptor his whole life. Instead of finding new ways to do art, he shut himself in the apartment and didn't even get dressed most days. He told my mom he couldn't stand the city anymore, couldn't take being unable to sculpt in the place where he'd had all his success. That's when they came up with the idea of moving to Prague. My dad needed drastic change, and my mom decided small-town living was the answer. Prague was just a four-hour drive from the city, not too far for my dad's monthly visits to the Genius. And so without consulting me, they made the decision that ruined my life.

• • •

I waited until I could breathe again, then walked into the store. My dad was up at the counter, his red hair streaked with silver, which was gleaming in the artificial light. I watched as he tried to get his wallet out to pay. His left leg was shaking, making it hard to slip his hand into his pocket. The clerk behind the counter, a young man with a scraggly beard, looked alarmed.

"To hell with it," my dad finally said, walking away on his stiff legs, the book left behind on the counter.

"Dad, can I help?" I asked softly as he passed me.

"No, I'm fine," he said, not even looking my way.

I slipped to the back of the store as he stalked out. I knew he would be okay getting home, but guilt still washed over me as I watched him go. A good daughter would at least try to walk home with him. But after what had happened last year at Friends, I didn't want any-one finding out about my dad. His brush-off gave me the excuse I needed.

The guilt ate at me as I paid for the book he'd wanted.

• • •

The next day after school I walked home and stood for a long time in front of our house. It was kind of cute if you like houses—a cottage, white with red trim. My mom was in the process of planting flowers around the ugly, oversize terra-cotta frog the last people living here had wisely abandoned. A series of flat stones marked a curved path up to the front porch, where a wicker rocking chair, also left by the last tenants, rocked in the breeze. It looked downright homey from the outside.

I dropped my bag on the porch and headed off for a walk. Nature had never been a favorite of mine, but I figured if I stayed on the road, I wouldn't have to tangle with it too much. And I needed something to fill up the empty hours before dinner.

As I walked out of town, the houses grew farther and farther apart. It was actually kind of pretty, with rolling hills, apple orchards, the occasional squirrel running by. The squawking birds were kind of annoying at first, but as I walked, I started to tune them out, or maybe they blended with the sound of farm equipment humming in the distance. I rounded a corner, and up ahead there was a picture-perfect farm:

the white clapboard house, the bright red barn with a silo, the white fence with horses grazing behind it. As I neared the house, a goose appeared in front of the barnyard and headed toward me.

I felt like a character in a book, walking up to Old MacDonald's farm. I gazed fondly at the goose, who was waddling toward me on its squat orange feet.

Suddenly the goose's fluffy little head jutted out in a threatening manner. Its wings started flapping, and it picked up speed so that it was actually running toward me. A deep hiss came from its throat. I backed up, but it kept coming, its wings pounding and the horrible hiss getting louder. I turned and ran as fast as I'd ever run, feeling the wind from the flapping wings following me.

"Help!" I shrieked, my last shred of dignity disappearing in the windstorm caused by the satanic goose. My feet pounded on the road and my breath came in shallow gasps. After a minute or two the hissing began to fade and the wind lessened. I kept going until I was sure the pursuit was over.

I stalked home, sweaty and utterly humili-ated.

"Hi, honey, where've you been?" my mother asked in her starched voice, which let me know that my dad was in one of his moods.

"I was attacked by a goose," I told her, walking into the kitchen to get a glass of water. I didn't necessarily expect her to get how upset-ting the whole thing had been, but I also didn't expect her to laugh. That's what she did, though—she sat down on one of the chairs at the table and let out a huge belly laugh.

I gave her the most poisonous look in my repertoire, but the laughter continued.

"A goose?" she choked out.

I stomped out of the kitchen. It's great to know that your mother is amused by an attempt on your life.

• • •

The following Monday I trudged up the steps to school and dragged myself through the front door. I'd spent the weekend cooped up in the house, unwilling to brave the country for fear some other farm animal was waiting to attack. Since I had no friends in Prague, I had no one to hang out with or call. Not that I wanted anyone to come over anyway. Ceese called once, but I just let the voice mail get it.

I tried to work up energy for my usual stride down the halls, but my heart wasn't in it. I watched people rushing around and greeting each other, guys high-fiving and girls shrieking. Over by my locker Sherry and her friends were bubbling about some party that they'd gone to on Saturday night. As they practically danced down the hall together, I decided it was time for a change—I needed a friend in Prague.

I felt a bit of my stride come back as I walked to class, looking around to see if there were any good friend candidates. I caught sight of two girls wearing passably cool clothes, but just as I walked by, they began shrieking and jumping up and down, so they were out. Anyone too perky wouldn't work—that was the last thing I needed at this point in my life.

The rest of the morning, the girls I passed all seemed to travel in packs, which I also ruled out—I didn't have the energy for a whole crowd. Finally, right before seventh period, as I was headed to chemistry, I spotted a strong candidate. She was scowling, and her clothes stood out as the only nonpastels in the hall. As I walked toward her, a beefy guy in a bright yellow football jersey came up behind her and covered her eyes. I'd seen this guy around—he had thick black hair and a pretty-boy face. Most of the girls swooned when he walked by. But this girl slapped his hands away and called him a jerk. He laughed, and her scowl deepened as she stomped down the hall.

Anyone with that much attitude had potential.

• • •

The next day I looked for her as soon as I got to school, but she wasn't in any of my classes. I hoped she wasn't absent—I was really ready to have someone to talk to. Finally at lunch I spotted her in a corner of the cafeteria, a book in one hand, a sandwich in the other. I strode over, hoping I looked more confident than I felt. Ceese and I met the first day of kindergarten and had been best friends ever since. Any other friends we hung out with, we met together. And even then, outgoing Ceese did the work and I just went along for the ride. Mostly, though, it was just the two of us and that was perfect. Until last year.

I felt my heart pounding as I reached the table. The girl didn't look up. I rubbed my sweaty palms on the sides of my dress as subtly as I could. Then I cleared my throat.

"Hey, can I sit here?"

She started and almost dropped her book, then looked up with her eyebrows raised. Her big brown eyes took in my black flapper dress and my pointy shoes. Then she nodded. "Sure."

I perched on the seat across from her. "I'm Matisse."

"I'm Violet." Her face was heart shaped with a tiny, upturned nose, and she had bouncy brown curls.

She closed her book, a volume of Pablo Neruda's poetry, and grinned at me. "You're new to this dump—I bet you'll hate it as much as I do in about a week."

"It's not possible to hate it any more than I

already do," I said as I settled back into my seat.

She nodded. "Well, be thankful you weren't trapped in Prague your whole life. I grew up here, if you can imagine anything more horrific. At least we're out of here in a few years."

"Two; and believe me, I'm counting." I opened my plastic container of angel hair pasta with pesto. "What's up with the name of the school? I can't even say it."

She rolled her eyes. "We call it Milo High because no one can say the actual name except the principal, and I think he had to take a class to learn. It's named for the son of the guy who founded Prague. He was kicked out of the real Prague for some reason and settled his family here. Too bad he didn't fall off a mountain on his way—would've saved us a lot of grief."

"He sounds like a loser. The real Prague is awesome." I wound some noodles around my fork.

"Wait, you've seriously been to Europe?"

I nodded, my mouth full.

"Oh, man, you're so lucky! I'd love to go there. Well, obviously I'd love to go anywhere that wasn't here. Where are you from?" She picked up her bottle of water and took a sip.

"New York City," I said, and Violet gasped.

"Oh, my God, you're kidding me! I'm totally going to New York the second I graduate! You're so lucky!" she said again. Then her forehead crinkled. "Oh, except you're not. You had to leave there to live here—that's gotta suck."

"It does. More than I can say." Though meeting her had already made things a lot better. "So, what are some other quirks of Prague?"

"This place is all about tradition—that's how I know about the jerk who founded it. That kind of stuff gets rammed down your throat at town festivals. We have a ton of those, especially celebrating the apples of Prague. This place is obsessed with its apples." Violet's upper lip curled in scorn. "And the big fall event is the hayride."

I felt my eyes go wide. "You absolutely have to be kidding me! A *hayride*? I thought that only happened in old movies!"

Violet giggled at my horror. "Yup—everyone gets all into it. And then there's a bonfire outside town where everyone drinks cider."

"Cider?"

"Fresh from the fabulous apple orchards of Prague." She wrinkled her nose. "It's pathetic. And don't even get me started on Czech Day, where we celebrate the town's heritage. Every year some idiot brings Chex mix."

I burst out laughing. "Chex mix to Czech Day—that is too much!"

Violet just shook her head.

All of a sudden, the pretty-boy football player from the day before walked up to our table and pulled out a chair. "What's got the new girl laughing so hard?" he asked Violet as he sat down.

Violet scowled as though a roach had walked across the table.

"Our little Violet's so funny, I'm sure she was just cracking you up," the guy said to me. Violet glared at him. "I'm Marco," he said, ignoring Violet and reaching his hand out to me.

"Matisse," I replied, not taking his hand. I wasn't getting chummy with an enemy of Violet's.

"Some welcome for your school's one and only starting quarterback!" Marco said, apparently not at all fazed by the cold reception he was receiving. He reached over and ruffled Violet's curls.

She ducked her head to get out of his reach, almost tipping her chair over. "Get lost, moron," she snapped.

"Aw, come on, Violet, you know you love me! I have that picture to prove it," Marco said.

"Sweetie." A sharp voice suddenly broke in. "We need to go make plans for the pep rally." A stunning blonde wearing a cheerleading uniform laid her pink frosted nails on Marco's shoulder. Violet looked at the table, her cheeks turning red.

The cheerleader turned to me. "Nice outfit," she said, her voice pure scorn.

"Yes, isn't it?" I replied, my tone icy.

"Okay, we're outa here," Marco said, standing up. "See you ladies later. Welcome to Milo, Matisse." He gave a casual wave as they walked away, the girl turning one last time to shoot us an acid look. I met her gaze with a nasty look of my own.

"Ugh," Violet groaned. "Meet Mr. and Ms. Milo High."

"What the hell?" I asked.

"Yeah, they really suck. That's Jennifer, the head cheerleader and bitch supreme of the school. Don't get on her bad side—she'll destroy your life."

I felt pretty confident some cheerleader from Backwater, USA, wasn't going to mess with me, but I was too interested in Marco's relationship with Violet to get into that. "What's the deal with him?"

"Marco, the school quarterback, class president, soon to be prom king, most popular guy in the universe. I can't stand him."

"He seems fond of you," I said. "He acted like you were best friends or something."

"Actually it's our moms who are best friends. We played together when we were little."

"What's the picture he's talking about?"

Violet looked like it was physically painful to think about. "It's this picture of us at the lake, when we were like four, and we're both naked, so he makes a big deal about it. He's such an imbecile, I can't even tell you."

"They're really quite the couple," I said.

"Oh, yeah."

The bell rang and we stood up. "What do you have now?" I asked.

"English," she said. "You?"

"History."

"I have the school magazine after school if you're interested in joining. It's pretty stupid, but I'm into writing and I figure it'll look good on my college applications."

"Thanks, but writing's not really my thing." I was happy that she'd asked, though. "What do you write for it?" We reached the doors to the cafeteria and waited while the kids in front of us went through.

"Features, sometimes, but mostly poetry. No one here really gets my stuff, but they publish it, so that's what counts."

"I think you'd have to worry if they actually did get it," I said as the crowd let up and we walked out into the hall.

Violet laughed. "So true." She stopped in

front of the science lab. "So I won't see you after school, but come sit with me at lunch tomorrow."

For a second I wondered why she didn't have anyone else to hang out with, but then I pushed the thought from my mind. She was probably just too cool for anyone in Prague. "Sounds great!"

Things were looking up.

Chapter Three

That night I was feeling cheerful as I went down to dinner. I set the table while my mom brought out the lasagna. Then we both sat down and waited for my dad. I fiddled with my fork, poking the tines into the woven tablecloth. My mom fussed with the salad, rooting out grape tomatoes from the bottom of the bowl and trying to get them to stay on top of the slippery bed of lettuce. Still no dad.

Finally my mom went to the doorway. "Blue, dinner!" she called.

It sounded out of place when she called him Blue here. Ever since I could remember, that was her special name for him, and he called her Lemon. Both names came from an Henri Matisse painting called *Blue Pot and Lemon* because that painting was the reason they'd met—and also the reason they'd named me Matisse. My mom was a grad student at the Sorbonne in Paris and my dad was teaching in London on a fellowship. They each spent their weekends visiting museums around Europe, and one snowy Saturday found them both at the Hermitage in St. Petersburg. My mom was in front of *Blue Pot and Lemon* when, as she tells it, a skinny guy with a wild beard stepped on her foot. My dad claims she stuck her foot out at the last minute and he had no way to avoid it. Regardless, she shrieked, he apologized, they discovered they were both native New Yorkers; and after a passionate discussion of *Blue Pot and Lemon*, they went out for pierogies and vodka.

"And the rest is history," my mom would always say. "If your dad wasn't such a klutz, we never would've met."

"You mean if you hadn't tried to trip me,"

my dad would say, laughing.

Now I couldn't remember the last time I'd heard my dad laugh, and as I looked across the table at my mom, I saw her face was creased with anxiety. He never called her Lemon anymore.

I heard the bedroom door slam and my dad's feet shuffle down the hall toward the dining room. He walked in slowly, his arms rigid by his sides, his face stiff, almost like a mask. He sat down a centimeter at a time, his body slowly sinking into the wooden chair. When he was settled, my mom served him a big portion of lasagna.

"That's too much," he said shortly.

"You always say that, honey, and then you always eat it. You love my lasagna," my mom cooed.

Actually, he'd never in his life told her she'd served him too much food. But my mom, determined to keep up the happy family façade, was ad-libbing like a pro.

She served me a plate and then took a generous portion for herself. We both ate, while my dad just sat.

"Go on, honey," my mom said, like he was a difficult three-year-old.

He reached for his fork, his hand traveling in slow motion. He managed to spear a piece of noodle, but by the time he got the fork up to his mouth, the food had slithered back onto his plate. He tried again, but the slippery noodles would not stay put.

I gulped down tasteless bites of lasagna, keeping my eyes on my plate so I wouldn't have to see my dad struggle to feed himself. The meal dragged and my mother chattered on, trying to act like everything was perfect.

"Damn," my dad said suddenly. He dropped his fork and pushed himself up off the chair, his hands gripping the sides of the table so hard, I worried it would tip. It took two tries before he was standing.

"Don, you aren't finished. You hardly had anything," my mom said.

My dad didn't even look at her. It was painful to watch him move out of the room like an old man, his feet barely getting off the ground. The bedroom door slammed a few minutes later.

My stomach was now a solid ball of cement. I set down my fork.

"How's the lasagna?" my mom asked, like nothing had happened.

"It was good," I said, pushing back my chair and bringing my plate to the sink. "I'm gonna go get some homework done."

I felt bad leaving my mom alone, but I couldn't bear to sit with her and play the everything-is-terrific game. It took too much out of me.

• • •

The following Monday I strode down the hall to my locker, my mind on the paper I was writing for my English class. In the past year my grades at Friends had slipped, but I could already tell it was going to take no effort to get A's here, which was a good thing because I wanted to get into a college far away from Prague. As I rounded the corner, the hick guy in overalls passed, his blond hair sticking up like he'd gotten caught in a severe windstorm.

"Hey there," he said, patting my arm.

I tried not to flinch at the unexpected touch.

People here were so weird—no one from home would ever touch someone they didn't know. I decided to ask Violet about him at lunch, to make sure he wasn't some stalker or something.

• • •

Violet was at our usual table, her water bottle and a half-eaten tuna sandwich in front of her.

"Hey," I said, pulling out the edamame I'd steamed the night before. But before I could ask her about the overalls hick, he was standing at the table.

"Hi, Hal," Violet said, acting like he was normal.

"Hey, Violet, how's it going?"

I took a closer look at Hal as he and Violet chatted. He had a large head with oversize features—it gave him kind of a goofy, puppy-dog look. His hair was even worse than it had been in the morning, because he'd mashed the front part down but the back still poked out in all directions. He had calluses on his large hands, and he was wearing muddy work boots. I wasn't impressed, but Violet was smiling at him, so I figured he couldn't be too bad.

"So, since we're next-door neighbors and I keep bumping into you, I figured it was time I introduced myself," Hal said, turning toward me, his blue eyes radiating warmth.

I felt like he'd just tossed a bucket of water over my head. I hadn't even thought to worry about someone from school living right next door. Had he seen my dad? Had he told people? "Hi," I replied shortly.

"You're Matisse, right? That's a great name. I love his paintings."

"Yeah," I muttered, glancing across the room so I wouldn't have to make eye contact. There was no way I was hanging out with anyone who could find out about my dad. Not after what had happened last year at Friends.

"So if you guys want any help with your yard or anything, just let me know."

Hal in my yard, meeting my parents? "We don't need help, thanks," I said quickly.

He paused for a second, then forged on. "Okay, well, let me know if you ever do. I've seen your grandparents a few times—it's cool you live with them."

Violet looked at me, her eyes wide with surprise. God, this guy was really an idiot. Just because people in New York City had their kids a little later than in Backwater, USA, he assumed that my parents were my grandparents.

"They're my parents," I said, my voice icy.

I heard Violet give a snort of laughter at his error.

"Sorry, God, that's so embarrassing, I just thought—I mean, I saw them and . . ." He fumbled, his face turning the color of one of Prague's finest apples.

I didn't reply; I just kept my eyes on him, my mouth a thin line.

"Well, this was a fiasco. I'm sorry." He turned and left, off to commit social blunders in other sections of the cafeteria, no doubt.

Violet finally stopped giggling. "Sorry, it's not really funny. It's just that he was hoping to be friends and he really stuck his foot in it."

"He's not someone I'd ever be friends with." I stuffed some edamame into my mouth. As I bit down, I realized I hadn't steamed them long enough—the beans were tough.

"Hal's not bad. Not like some people around here." Her face hardened for a moment; then she shook her head. "I shouldn't have laughed at him; I probably hurt his feelings. Seriously, he's a sweet guy."

"But he walks around in overalls," I said, even though it wasn't the real reason I now hated him.

"Yeah, well, he works on one of the farms."

No doubt the one with the satanic goose.

"He wants to be an organic farmer. He's all into environmental stuff and also Buddhism," she said.

"How do farming and Buddhism go together?"

"I don't know; you'd have to ask him. But it's kind of neat. His parents are these total business types, pretty conservative, and Hal's just doing his own thing."

No matter how cool Hal was, he was officially on top of my "To Be Avoided at All Costs" list. So I changed the subject back to the many lame features of Milo High, in hopes that lunch wouldn't be completely ruined.

But as Violet told me about last year's year-book, with its "Pride of Prague" theme, I couldn't get Hal's words out of my head. *I've seen your grandparents a few times.* What exactly had he seen? And what would he see if he started nosing around?

• • •

That night I got an email from Ceese.

> Tisse,
> I miss you tons!!!! James and I blah blah blah blah blah blah blah blah blah blah. Blah blah blah blah blah blah blah blah blah blah blah blah blah blah blah.
> How's your dad? How are you doing? I think blah blah blah blah blah blah blah. Blah blah blah blah blah blah blah blah blah.
> Ceese, Missing you in NYC

We'd been best friends for so long, I couldn't believe I actually felt my skin crawl reading, or rather not reading, her email.

I met Ceese the first day of kindergarten at Friends. I had been dropped off by my dad and was sitting alone on the "playtime mat." All the students were supposed to be sitting on the playtime mat, but Darryl Smith had somehow opened the teacher's terrarium and three frogs and an unknown number of crickets escaped, causing a mini riot to break out. All the other kids were happily chasing the escaped animals, and no one noticed when a plump little girl with wild copper curls marched into the classroom.

"What are they doing?" she asked me.

"Chasing frogs and crickets."

"Why aren't you chasing them?"

"Frogs and crickets are stupid," I replied.

"Yeah," she said, nodding like I'd said something brilliant. She sat down next to me, neatly tucking her bright yellow dress under her. "Boys are stupid too."

"Yeah," I said, and that was that. We shortened our names and became Ceese (short for Cecile) and Tisse, best friends joined at the hip. I was there when her parents split; she was there when my grandma died; we had our first crushes together; we survived our first breakups together, and nothing in my life felt real until Ceese and I had talked it over. We even had the future set—we were both applying to Oxford University and would spend four years traveling around Europe; then we'd return to NYC, where we'd move into lofts next door to each other and start thrilling careers. We weren't quite sure what those would be yet, but they would be fabulous and so would our lives together.

And then last year happened. It all started with James, the new guy from Montreal. Ceese took one look at his long blond hair and surly expression, and she was in love. This wasn't unusual—Ceese fell in and out of love on a daily basis, and bad-boy types like James were her obsession. James naturally fell for her too—Ceese's curls were soft ringlets, her freckles were now just a soft dusting on a gorgeous face, and her plump little-girl body had grown into perfect curves. Ceese wailed that she was fat, but guys were always flocking to her. James was just like all the rest, totally smitten. And Ceese raved endlessly about how perfect they were together, just like she always did. But then one day it wasn't just like it always was—something had shifted. I first noticed it when James would know things about Ceese's life before I did. Like she called him first when her dad started dating a twenty-year-old model named Licorice and he told her to call him Gabe because "Dad" made him feel old. She acted like it was no big deal that she didn't tell me first, but it was. Guys came and went, but we had always been first for each other. More and more, now, it was James first, and me second. When I complained to Ceese about it, she said it was my fault, that I was pushing her away because I wouldn't talk about my dad.

That was the other thing—she was always nagging me to talk about my dad. But the truth was, there was nothing to discuss. Yes, his symptoms were getting worse; yes, his meds had more off periods; yes, he was upset about it. But it was the last thing in the world I wanted to talk about. And Ceese just wouldn't leave it alone; she kept on me about it, asking how I felt, what was going on, how my mom was doing. It got old.

And so it totally infuriated me that she'd accused me of being the one to sabotage our friendship, when really it was her, prying about my dad and spending all her time with James. By the end of the year it was the "Ceese and James Show," and I was a minor character off to the side. Still, she got all upset when I told her we were moving, like we were still best friends, like she'd even notice I was gone.

And now this email, where it was all the same thing: James and irritating questions about my dad.

I deleted the message and turned off the computer.

Chapter Four

When I got home the next day, there was a large brown spider on the kitchen table, right where I'd planned to eat a snack. I screamed and raced out of the room to find my mom. My dad and I were total insect wimps, but my mom had gone to summer camp when she was young, and she wasn't afraid to relocate insects from our living space back into nature. Of course, at home that just meant dealing with the occasional water bug, but on vacations I'd seen her track down beetles, spiders, and once even a large centipede.

She wasn't in the living room, so I ran up

the attic stairs to her studio. No Mom. And then I stopped short, taking in the whole room. It was immaculate. Her brushes were neatly tucked inside jars by the sink, her paints were in careful rows on her storage table, her pallets were stacked next to them, and her canvases were in their racks. On her easel sat one blank canvas.

I sucked in my breath. My body felt chilled. Normally canvases were everywhere, pallets and brushes were spread across the table, and her work space was surrounded by half-used tubes of paint. Most important, the canvas on her easel was never blank. She was always working on *something*.

This whole time she'd been acting like things were fine and she was doing great. But as I looked around the pristine studio, I wondered if she was even just okay.

I *needed* my mom to be okay.

I stared for another moment at the empty canvas. Then I left her studio, pulling the door firmly closed behind me.

• • •

Two days later Violet and I were sitting in the cafeteria happily snarking about the cheerleading squad. I was peeling an Italian blood orange from the crate my mom ordered every fall from Williams-Sonoma, and Violet was slurping from her bottle of water.

"Vacuous dolls," she said with a sniff.

I noticed Jennifer in a teensy tank top and Daisy Dukes, running her fingers through Marco's hair. "She's the worst of the bunch," I told Violet, who knew exactly who I meant. "She's entirely plastic."

"Yup." Violet nodded. "That's who my sister aspires to be."

"You can't be serious!" I didn't even know Violet had a sister. "How could someone with your DNA want to be like *that*?"

"Well, she's only in seventh grade, but she makes my parents take her to gymnastics class so she can make the squad when she's a freshman. She even wants to dye her hair blond."

"That's totally gross. You're her big sister— can't you guide her or something?"

Violet shook her head. "She doesn't listen to

me. She thinks I'm a total dork because I read poetry and want to go to college. She wants to become a Laker Girl."

"Well, she's young—there's still hope." I finished peeling my orange and began separating it into sections.

"Maybe. Do you have any brothers or sisters?"

I popped a section of orange into my mouth and shook my head.

"Lucky," she said. "My mom's totally proud of my sister. They're always off shopping for clothes and makeup together. I'm like the freak of the family."

"No, you're the normal one."

"Try telling them that," she said. "What about you and your mom—do you guys get along?"

"Sure," I said dismissively.

"What does she do?"

"She's a painter." I pulled off a section of my orange a little too hard, and it split open.

"No way, that's so cool!" Violet was suddenly all animated. "Does she sell her stuff?"

"Yeah." My tone was curt.

"No way! Is she, like, famous?"

I shrugged.

"What does your dad do?" she asked.

That was a place I wasn't going. "Oh my God, look what Jennifer is doing!"

Violet gave me an odd look, since all Jennifer was doing was combing her hair, but she seemed to take the hint and dropped her line of questioning.

I felt bad, but I couldn't risk it. When everyone at Friends found out about my dad, it was like I became a different person. I was no longer just Matisse; I was "poor Matisse," girl-with-a-sick-father. Half the people at school were either in therapy or had therapists as parents, so they all wanted to "help me talk about it." Each day I had to steel myself for the pitying glances and ongoing discussions about my dad, talks I shut down as fast as I could. After two weeks of "thoughtful" questions and "empathetic" stories, I was ready to throw myself off the Brooklyn Bridge. The thing was, I wanted to talk about everything and anything *except* my dad.

When my dad got his PD diagnosis and we knew for sure he would never get better, just slowly get worse, a wound, huge and raw, opened up inside me. And last year, as my dad started to succumb to symptoms, that wound became infected. For a couple of days I was a total mess, but then it was like the wound got covered over by a layer of hard scar tissue that sealed it off. As long as I didn't think too much about my dad, I was okay. But anything that reminded me about the PD pressed on the wound and made me feel like I was going to explode. If I hadn't started snapping people's heads off when they asked about my dad, I probably would've been carted off to Bellevue before the new year.

The one thing Prague had going for it was that no one knew about my dad. After his one foray into the bookstore in town, he had decided to stay put. All I had to do was keep Hal and Violet and everyone else away. And then maybe I could survive this year.

• • •

When I got home, there was another email from Ceese waiting for me. This one was called Forever Yours. In eighth grade Ceese and I had decided to find music groups that illustrated our style. We raided her dad's record and tape collection and went old school. After many hours of listening, Ceese decided that she was a Journey girl, and I found that the disco rhythms of ABBA were about the greatest thing I'd ever heard. We went on missions to thrift stores to find T-shirts from "our" bands and collected all their albums, which luckily came on CD's. We used to quote lines from songs at appropriate moments, but we'd stopped doing it last year, after James, though ABBA was still the first music I put on when I was feeling really bad. But Ceese seemed to be reviving it, quoting Journey's "Forever Yours," pretending we were still real best friends.

I opened the email and wasn't surprised to see it contained the usual: James prattle, and prying about my dad. But then at the end there was a threat: "I'm planning a road trip up there if I don't hear from you—I'm worried." She signed it "Happy and in love in NYC," so she couldn't be too worried. But I was scared anyway—the last thing I needed to deal with was Ceese in Prague. So I drummed up an email.

> Ceese,
> Glad to hear all is well in the Big Apple. Hey to everyone at Friends. The country sucks, but I met some cool people at school so that's good. Gotta go eat—write more later.
> Tisse, alive and well in Prague, New York

There were only two blatant lies in it. I wasn't glad to hear all was well in the Big Apple, and I had no plans to go eat. The rest was a bit of truth stretching: I had met one cool person, and I was alive and well—as in I wasn't dead. I sent it, hoping she'd put off taking any drastic action for a while.

• • •

At 5:58 that night I had a silent debate with myself. Back before my dad got sick, we used to watch the news together once or twice a week. We'd make fun of how seriously the newscasters took themselves, and then during commercials we'd make up stories, like a report about a woman who lost a sock in a Laundromat or a guy who was on trial for killing roaches. My dad would act them out, totally hamming it up, and I'd be hysterical. My favorite was his imitation of this guy who did the weather on a local channel. My dad called him Hair Plugs because he had these sprouts of hair over the crown of his head that he was constantly running his hands through as he spoke in a syrupy voice about incoming storms.

"Tonight we'll see quite a drop in temperature," my dad would say, holding his glass of juice or wine as a microphone in one hand and running his other hand through his hair, just like Hair Plugs did. "Get out those winter jackets because you'll—oh no, not my hair!" he'd howl, acting as though he'd just ripped out a clump of hair-plug hair. "This is a dire medical emergency! I need to replace my hair!"

At this point I'd be on the floor laughing. My dad would be running around the room, his hands on his head. "Who cares about the weather—this is a crisis!" he'd shout.

"Blue, really, you're going to disturb the neighbors," my mom would say, coming in from the kitchen where she was going through take-out menus. But she would be laughing too.

We'd stopped watching once he got sick, but I'd been thinking maybe we should start again. When we first got to Prague, I was too pissed at him and my mom to even consider it. But now that I'd met Violet and things weren't totally wretched, I thought it might be fun.

So I pushed myself up out of my desk chair and went to my parents' bedroom. I could hear the TV blaring behind the closed door. Back home we had only one TV, which was in the living room and almost never on. But my dad had gotten another set when we moved here and installed it in the bedroom. It had been on non-stop the past few weeks.

I had to knock twice before he heard.

"What?" he called.

"It's me. I thought maybe we could watch the news," I said.

There was a pause. "Okay, come on in."

I walked in and tripped over his slippers, which were lying just inside the door. There were clothes draped on the chair and dressers, and the hamper was overflowing. My mom was usually a drill sergeant about tidiness, and for a second it felt like I'd walked into the wrong bedroom.

My dad was lying on the bed, his head propped up on pillows and the remote in his hand. He was wearing the same maroon sweats he'd had on all week. Back home he hadn't even owned a pair of sweats. The TV was tuned to some dumb sitcom from the nineties, and my dad, who once scorned TV as a waste of time, appeared riveted. But when I came and settled on the bed, he changed the channel to the news.

I tried not to notice his left arm jerking and twitching as it lay on the comforter. The tremors were the worst when he was still.

We stared silently as the overly made up anchorwoman finished up a story about a car accident on the highway. Her phony concern was the sort of thing we usually mocked.

"All right, Bob. Now why don't you give us that weather update," she said, suddenly formidably cheery.

I laughed and after a minute my dad joined in. Kind of.

The weather guy had a sugary voice and a pasted-on smile. He was perfect fodder for my dad's imitation. But when the commercials came, my dad remained silent. We watched as a housewife raved about laundry soap and a stunt driver made a Toyota look like the answer to eternal happiness. Then came a commercial for an international cell phone company that showed a woman calling her elderly father to wish him a happy birthday from a temple in India. As the dad beamed, overjoyed that she had been able to make the call, I felt my throat tighten.

The news came on again, and the overly made up anchorwoman was back to tell us about a robbery that had taken place in Ithaca. I glanced over at my dad. He was gazing at the screen, his face tight, and I could tell he wasn't hearing a word.

"The news here isn't that great," I said, getting up.

"We can keep watching," he said. It was obvious he didn't care one way or the other.

"No, I have homework," I said.

I heard the canned laughter of a sitcom blaring as I closed the bedroom door.

• • •

Friday morning as I walked down the hall to my locker, I saw a guy and a girl in matching Milo High sweatshirts making out by the water fountain. A couple in front of me held hands and swung them as they walked to class. And when I got to my locker, Sherry was there with a guy. He was telling her about some big-deal thing he'd done in the last football game, and she was cooing with admiration. Although Sherry was making a fool of of herself, the sight of all the couples inspired me: I needed a boy. Someone to take my mind off how much my life sucked.

• • •

"I need to find a guy," I announced to Violet as I pulled a chair up to our table and set my spinach salad down.

 54

"Yeah?" Violet asked, her eyebrows knitting together.

"Yeah. I need some romance to spice up my life," I said.

"That makes sense," she said.

"Who've you dated here?"

Violet waved dismissively. "No one, really. I went to a dance in ninth grade with this guy Stan who played chess. It was okay—not really a date though. Did you date a lot in the city?" She took a bite of her cafeteria pizza.

"Yup. There were some really cool guys at my old school." I sighed wistfully.

"Yeah?" She seemed interested, so I went on.

"My freshman year I was with this guy Raven. He surfed and—"

"Wait, who surfs in New York City?"

"Before we got together he spent the summer in Brazil and surfed like every day." I smiled, remembering how good he looked that first day back at school, his long blond hair baked a white gold, and those awesome surfing muscles he'd developed. "We had some good times."

"What'd you do?"

"We mostly went to parties and made out."
I felt toasty warm just thinking about it. "He
was the best kisser."

Violet's cheeks turned pink but she laughed.
"So, were you in love with Raven?"

"No, we weren't soul mates or anything."

Guys were for fun, for making out, for making me feel good. Ceese was for real talking, at
least until she got all into James.

"But then you didn't date anyone last year?"

I frowned. Of course I hadn't dated anyone
last year. All anyone at Friends could talk about
was my dad, and I didn't need some oversensitive
guy trying to "be there" for me. "No, by then all
the guys were old news."

"Well, then it's just a question of finding
someone here worth your time," she said, and I
nodded.

• • •

I looked around for the next few days but saw
no one even remotely interesting. I knew there
had to be a gem hidden somewhere in all the
gravel, though.

Wednesday morning I was strolling up the path to school when the toe of my boot caught a crack in the sidewalk and I stumbled, almost falling. I cursed loudly. As I regained my balance and dignity, I noticed a guy sitting on the grass, slightly apart from the groups of kids talking and laughing on the lawn in front of Milo. He was wearing a black T-shirt that said THE REVOLUTION WILL NOT BE TELEVISED and beat-up jeans. His spiky black hair was wilting in the humidity, and he had a tattoo on one arm. He was reading the local paper with a scowl on his face.

A bubbly feeling of anticipation filled my belly. Ceese wasn't the only one who liked bad boys.

Chapter Five

"So I found him." I'd arrived at our table before Violet and had been eagerly waiting to see what she knew about my potential new boyfriend.

She set down her water and sandwich and flopped into a chair. "Okay, I'm ready."

"Hot, black spiky hair, tall, looks like he has attitude."

Violet was nodding. "Sure, that's Dylan. Well, he makes everyone call him Dylan, after Bob Dylan. His real name is a secret." She began ticking off facts about him. "He just started school here last year—before that he

58

was in boarding school. He's totally political, always organizing demonstrations and passing out information on workers' rights violations and foods we should boycott and stuff. His folks are rich, but he acts like he's one of the oppressed. Not a bad guy, just very intense."

"Is he dating anyone?"

"I don't think so, not unless he hooked up with someone over the summer, but I doubt it. He's too focused on his causes." Violet took a sip of water. "Last year he dated this girl Brooke, but it didn't last very long."

"What's she like?"

"Smart and pretty like you."

I smiled. Violet knew just the right thing to say. "So how am I going to meet him?"

"Get involved in one of his causes. That has to be the fastest way to his heart."

Before I could ask for some specifics on his causes, Marco arrived at our table.

"You can't sit here," Violet said before he could say anything.

Marco pulled out a chair. "Sure I can." He sat. Violet and I both glared at him.

"You *can*. The point is that you're not wanted here." Violet crossed her arms over her chest.

Marco laughed. "Sure you want me, you both do!"

Violet made a vomiting sound.

"So—are you ladies coming to the pep rally Friday? We've got a big game against Milford, and we need your support."

"Yeah, of course we'll be there! I'm coming right after I trade in my brain for a watermelon!" Violet said, doing a great cheerleader imitation.

I laughed, and to my surprise Marco snickered appreciatively. I almost smiled at him but caught myself in time.

I was about to make a cutting remark when I saw Jennifer march up, her expression pure poison. That girl's hate packed a punch. When Violet spotted Jennifer, she sagged in her seat and dropped her eyes. Marco looked puzzled— he was the only one who hadn't noticed his demon girlfriend approaching.

"Hey, Marco, come back to the table," she

said, coming up behind him. Her voice was coy but her look was venomous.

I kept my expression even, meeting her gaze until she looked away.

"I'm counting on you guys for Friday," Marco said as he and Jennifer laced their fingers together for the long trek back to the popular table.

"God, he's infuriating," Violet muttered, shredding the label on her water bottle.

"Yeah," I agreed, though despite myself I was starting to get a kick out of Marco. He always seemed tickled by Violet's barbs, which was endearing. And as I looked more closely, I realized he was actually pretty cute.

"I can't stand him. Can you imagine, asking us to go to the pep rally? I'd rather slit my wrists!"

"What is a pep rally, anyway?"

"Okay, you went to the coolest school in the world if you didn't have pep rallies. After school everyone sits on the bleachers, waving pom-poms, and the school band plays and the cheer-leaders cheer and the team runs out and everyone yells. Then the coach and some players talk and everyone yells more. Then you go home." Violet shook her head in disgust. "There's not a bigger waste of time out there. Well, except maybe the game itself."

"What's the point?"

"To get the team psyched up or something."

"But why would anyone care if they were psyched up or not?"

Violet spread out her hands. "That's the mystery."

The bell rang and we started walking out of the cafeteria. I still hadn't seen Dylan. "Tomorrow we need to come up with a plan for me to meet my new boyfriend," I told Violet.

"You got it," she said.

● ● ●

The next day I was obsessed with finding Dylan. I didn't see him before school, though I lingered on the lawn until the warning bell rang. I didn't see him in the halls between classes, and by lunch I was feeling a little desperate.

"He's nowhere," I whined to Violet as I threw my stuff down on the table.

"Hi to you too," she said, her eyes twinkling. "Don't worry, I'm on it. He eats out back on the patio."

"I didn't even know there *was* a patio," I said, grabbing my stuff. "Let's go."

"Well, it's called a patio," Violet said, standing up. "It's more like a patch of concrete with a few picnic benches on it."

We walked out of the cafeteria, down the main hall, and through a big metal door. The patio was just as Violet had described, though she'd neglected to mention the view of the parking lot and stench of the Dumpsters a few feet away.

But the important thing was Dylan, and there he was, perched on a table, writing in a notebook on his lap. Violet and I sat down at a table nearby.

"So what are you going to do?" she asked.

I suddenly realized that I wasn't sure. This was the part of getting a guy that Ceese had always advised me on. She had the best opening lines ever, and she always got me pumped up. I guess you could say she was a one-woman pep rally, psyching me up for the game.

I took a deep breath. "I'm going to talk to him." I didn't need Ceese. I could do this on my own.

"But what will you say?" Violet asked.

I stood up. "I'll figure it out on the way over."

I tossed my hair, straightened my dress, and glided over to Dylan. He didn't look up. I stood next to him, was completely ignored, and suddenly wondered if I really did need Ceese's help to get a guy.

"Hi," I blurted out, a little too loudly.

Dylan jumped. The notebook slipped off his lap, and we both reached for it as it fell to the ground.

"Sorry about that. I'm Matisse."

Dylan gave me a slow smile. "Matisse, I've seen you around." He picked up the notebook, then sat back on the table. "Would you like to join me?"

I stepped lightly up on the bench and settled beside him on the table.

"You've seen me, huh?" I gave my hair another toss, this time a little too vigorously, and the ends of it whipped into my eyes, making them water. Luckily Dylan didn't seem to notice.

"You stand out, and I mean that in a good way. You're so not from around here, are you?"

"I just moved from New York City."

Dylan's eyes lit up. "Man, I'd love to live there. You've got some real action going on in New York City, people trying to make a difference."

"Yup." I wasn't superpolitical, but I'd been active in Amnesty International and world peace stuff. Most of us at Friends were.

"That's the place to really get things started, with all the rich bastards, you know?" His eyes flashed as he spoke.

"Definitely," I said, admiring how cute he was when he got worked up. "Welfare cuts have caused a lot of problems," I added.

He punched his fist into his palm. "The damn politicians don't know anything about the real world, what the people struggle with. That's what we need to change. Do you know the Food Wagon?"

It seemed like a non sequitur, but I nodded. The Food Wagon was the big grocery store in town.

"Do your parents shop there?" He didn't wait for an answer. "Because they need to stop. Now. The workers are being totally exploited—they get minimum wage and no benefits. The people of Prague need to say 'no more.'"

I was starting to get a little bored by his lecture, so I tuned it out and focused on him. He wore a white T-shirt with a hole in the left sleeve. There was a rip in the knee of his green cords and he wore black Converse high-tops. I was close enough to read the tattoo on his arm. It said, not surprisingly, *Revolution*. As he went on about wages and injustice, I watched his lips move and imagined kissing him.

"All right, enough about that." He ran his fingers through his hair, making the black spikes stand up straight. "Tell me about you."

I leaned forward, ready to dazzle him.

But then the bell rang. We stood up.

"Listen, I'm leading a demonstration at the Food Wagon next week, on Tuesday. Come by."

"I will." I fluttered my fingers at him, then watched as he headed into school. I practically ran over to Violet, who was waiting at our table. "He asked me out!"

"Oh my God, really?"

"Well, he asked me to go to a demonstration on Tuesday. It's not a date, but it'll lead to one."

We walked back through the doors and into the crowded hallway.

I touched Violet's shoulder. "Listen, I won't ditch you for lunch again. It was a one-time thing, to get things started with Dylan." I wanted her to know straight off that I wasn't the Ceese type of girl.

Violet's eyes narrowed and her lips curled down. "You don't seem the type to dump friends . . . but you can never tell."

"I'm definitely not." It was weird that she put it that way. Even Ceese didn't dump me— she'd just put her relationship with James first.

Pleased with my victory, I headed off to my locker. On the way I passed Hal the Hick, who glanced at me. I ignored him and he looked away. Maybe he'd finally gotten the message.

Chapter Six

The next day it was raining, and even though my house was only about six blocks from school, I was soaking wet by the time I arrived. My polka-dot raincoat, while fashionable, was not effective at keeping the drops out, so I walked into school feeling foul. I noticed most people here carried colorful umbrellas, which figured: at home not even the biggest geeks at Friends would be caught dead carrying umbrellas in any shade but black. But at Milo it was probably cool. I walked down the hall to my locker, my polka-dot rain boots leaving little puddles as I went.

I rounded the corner, and next to the gaggle of Sherry's friends, who always seemed to congregate for a morning squeal fest, was an agitated Violet. She was tugging at a curl so ferociously that I wouldn't have been surprised to see it pop off her head, and her mouth was pursed so tightly, she had a white ring around her lips. When she saw me, she began waving frantically.

"Oh, thank God you're here! Matisse, you're not going to believe it." Her voice was sharp with outrage. "You know that idiotic pep rally? I have to cover it for the magazine!"

"No way!"

"Yup." She pursed her lips, and her words came out clipped. "I tried to get out of it, but Paul, our moron editor, said I had to, that I would bring a fresh perspective or some crap like that."

I shook my head and made sympathetic sounds as I wrestled with the stuff in my locker. When I'd finally tugged out my chem book, I noticed one of Sherry's gaggle smirking in Violet's direction and nudging an identical-looking girl, as though they were laughing at some kind of joke. "Something funny?" I asked her loudly.

The girl turned to me, her eyebrows raised and her mouth open, like she was ready to tell me off. But when she saw my face, her mouth snapped shut and she shook her head.

"Yeah, I didn't think so," I told her, slamming my locker shut. "Let's go," I said to Violet.

"Man, you never let anyone get away with anything," she said as we headed to the stairs. The warning bell rang and kids moved faster, some pushing against us as we started up the stairs. "Oh, my God," Violet exclaimed, stopping short and grabbing my arm. The girl behind me stepped on my heel, and I pulled Violet forward.

"What?" I asked, as we started up the stairs again.

"I've got it—I know how I can get through this pep rally! You can come with me!" She clapped her hands together, her eyes bright.

We reached the top of the stairs, and I craned my neck back to check if my boot had

70

gotten scuffed. "Sorry, Violet, but I'd rather eat ground-up glass."

"Please, Matisse, I'll die if I have to go alone! If we're both there, we can make fun of everyone."

Violet's eyes were wide, and she radiated desperation. I remembered how intimidated she was by bitch queens like Jennifer, and I thought of how much better my life at Milo was now that we were friends. It would suck, but of course I'd do it. "All right, but we're not staying long. Half an hour, tops."

"Thank you, thank you, thank you! I am forever indebted to you," she bubbled.

"Don't worry about it," I said, laughing. The late bell rang and we started toward our home-rooms.

"It's right after school, in the gym," she called.

• • •

When we walked into the gym after school, the place was mobbed. The bleachers on both sides were crammed with shouting people. More than half of them were wearing yellow Milo

High T-shirts. A bunch had yellow-and-white pom-poms that they were already waving, and a sad little band in the corner played the Milo fight song, slightly out of sync and very off-key. Seemingly they knew no other song, because once they finished the fight song, they took a ten-second break and started it up again.

"This sucks," I told Violet. In her black T-shirt and baggy jeans, she stood out like a city girl in a cornfield. I was wearing an espresso-colored catsuit I'd found at Andy's Cheapees in Greenwich Village, a look that was probably never before seen in Prague.

"Tell me about it." Violet was squinting, as though the scene in front of her was too much to take in all at once. She carried a notebook and pen. "Let's sit." She seemed eager to melt into the crowd.

"How about we just lurk by the door? Then we can get the hell out of here when you've found enough to write about." There was no way I was climbing into those bleachers.

"Good idea."

We leaned against the wall, with a clear view

of the podium set up near the back of the gym. I pulled a nail file out of my bag, and Violet flipped open her notebook.

Principal Stern walked up to the podium. "Can you hear me?" he asked, just as a rush of feedback screamed through the microphone. A loud howl of protest filled the auditorium. He adjusted something. "All right, I think we've got it now. Welcome, everyone! It's great to see all of you here to support Milo! This is a big game, and we want to get out there and beat Milford." People booed at the mention of the other team. "Students of Milo High, I give you your football team!"

A door next to the podium burst open, and the team, in their ridiculous yellow uniforms, ran out and did a lap around the gym as the student body went mad with excitement. People shouted and clapped and cheered, waving their stupid pom-poms as though it were a rock concert. The players pumped their fists as they ran. Marco was in the lead, and when they got closer to us, I heard Violet groan. She tried to duck behind me, but as he neared, Marco caught sight of both of us. He gave us a thumbs-up.

"Knew you guys wouldn't miss it!" he shouted as he ran by. Everyone had reached out to slap hands with the team except me and Violet.

"Jerk," she muttered.

I put all my attention on sweeping the file down the side of my pinky nail so that I wouldn't laugh—Marco really was kind of funny. His moves were cocky, but there was something about how he did things that told you he didn't take any of it that seriously—maybe it was his smile and the way he laughed.

The cheerleaders had now run out to the center of the gym and were performing a complicated routine that culminated in a pyramid with a glowing Jennifer at the top.

"I hope they implode," I told Violet.

But the pyramid came apart flawlessly, Jennifer leaping off in a somersault and landing effortlessly on her toes. She gave a peppy wave to the crowd, and the cheers grew even louder. I feared for my hearing.

My nails were done, so I tucked my file back

into my bag. As I looked up to see what idiotic event came next, I accidentally made eye contact with Hal the Hick, who was sandwiched between two cutesy girls in yellow Milo shirts. One had her arm resting across Hal's shoulder. He waved and I looked away quickly.

The team trotted up to the podium, and the coach rushed to the microphone. But somehow it had stopped functioning, so all we saw was his mouth moving. A wave of laughter echoed around the gym as the principal raced up to try to fix the problem.

I was idly enjoying his discomfort when I heard a sharp intake of breath from Violet. I turned and saw the cheerleaders, led by Jennifer, walking straight toward us. The people around us grew silent as the golden group approached.

Jennifer's hands were on her tiny waist. "So, Violet and Matisse," she said, making my name sound like a toxic chemical, "what brings you two losers here?"

Beside me Violet seemed to have shrunk. Her head hung down and her body was curled in.

But no one called me a loser and got away with it.

"We were in the mood for some comedy. I thought this stuff went out with drive-in movies and dates at the soda shoppe, but you're so backward, you still actually think it's cool." My voice was louder than I'd intended, and I heard someone gasp.

"Cheerleading is cool everywhere!" Jennifer snapped.

"Where things actually matter, it's a total joke—kind of like you." It was deeply satisfying to tell her off.

Her face turned red, and she was gathering steam for a retort, when suddenly the mike went back on and the coach's voice came booming through. "Let's have a big hand for our terrific cheerleaders!" he yelled.

One of the clones in a cheerleading outfit reached out and gently pulled Jennifer up toward the podium with the rest of the group. I waved good-bye.

"Uh-oh, you shouldn't have done that," Violet whispered.

"What do you mean?" I asked. "Why not?"

"Let's not talk about it here," she whispered, glancing around as though she feared we'd be overheard.

"What, do the cheerleaders have a secret police force?" I asked.

Violet grabbed my arm and dragged me through the double doors. I noticed several people looking at us as we left. Cheerleader secret agents, no doubt.

Out in the hall Violet turned to me. "I'm serious about her, Matisse—she's vicious." Violet was tugging on a curl. "You don't know the lengths she'll go to to humiliate someone, and what you just said to her—she's not going to forget it."

"Good! I don't want her to! She can't just treat people like that." I was annoyed at Violet. "I don't understand why you let her intimidate you. She only has power if you give it to her."

Violet's face was creased with anxiety. "You just don't get it."

I didn't, not at all.

"She can really hurt you if you're not careful."

Before I could tell her how dumb that was, one of the gym doors opened and two girls walked out. One was short and heavy, with huge green eyes. The other was tall, with bad skin and long chestnut hair. Next to me I heard a rustling sound, and I turned to see Violet fleeing down the hall. I glanced back at the two girls, who were leaning close together, whispering as they watched Violet go.

I ran to catch up with Violet, who was already outside the building. "Hey, what's going on?" I asked her.

Violet shook her head. "Nothing. I just don't like them."

Her hands were curled into fists. There was clearly more to it than that.

"Are you sure that's it?" I asked.

"Yes," she snapped, then immediately looked guilty. "Sorry, I just . . ." She glanced behind us, then started walking down the path. "Listen, do you want to come over to my house and hang out?"

She clearly wanted to talk about it in a more private setting. But an invite to her house would mean I'd have to invite her to mine at some point. And as much as I wanted to be a good friend, I couldn't do it. "Maybe another time— I should get home."

Violet stared at her shoe as she traced a line in the dirt path. "Whatever. See you Monday. And thanks again for coming with me to the rally." Her voice was flat and I winced. I'd let her down. But I couldn't see any other way around it. It was just too risky.

As I walked toward my house, I glanced back at Violet. Her shoulders were stiff and her walk was brisk. For a second I thought how easy it would be to catch up with her.

And then I turned and headed home.

• • •

That night I got another email from Ceese. She went on and on about the play Friends was putting on this year, written by none other than James. It sounded like a cross between Shakespeare and an interpretive dance—very typical of Friends. And very far from the world of pep rallies and bitchy cheerleaders. I didn't write back.

• • •

On Monday when I got home from school, my mom was out in the front yard, digging. A bunch of disgusting-looking onionlike things sat in a tray next to her. She was wearing a big, floppy straw hat and looked like a photo from *Country Bumpkin Gardeners USA*. The lines on her face stood out, as though every muscle was tense. I felt my stomach twist.

"Hi, honey," she called as I approached.

"What are you doing?" I asked.

"Planting bulbs," she said, gesturing to the filthy onion things.

"To grow onions?"

"No, for flowers," she said, laughing a little.

"That'll be nice."

She nodded, her face relaxing a bit. "How was school?"

"Pretty sucky," I said, leaning against the porch.

"Well, I hope you're meeting some people you like, because I had this really great idea today."

"What is it?" I asked, ready to hear how I

should bake cupcakes for my class or something.

"We should throw a big party for Dad's sixtieth birthday next month! We can invite all our new friends and all our friends from the city—it'll be a blast!" She beamed.

I felt like she'd just dumped a pile of dirt over my head. What planet did she live on? My dad barely spent time in the same room as us—did she really think he'd like a houseful of people to celebrate his birthday? Because he certainly had nothing to celebrate.

She was still looking at me, the smile shellacked across her face. "So what do you think, honey?"

"I think that's the worst idea I've heard in my entire life," I snapped.

"I don't know what you mean—it'll be fun."

I looked at her grimace of a smile, the dark circles under her eyes, her fingers clenched around the shovel. This was not my mom. My mom used to talk about things when she was upset, and listen to me when I was. She was the one who taught me how to put on makeup and where to kick a guy if he got fresh. I'd cried to her the night I got dumped by Von Gordon, and she hadn't told me everything would be fine. She'd listened and commiserated and made me a coffee milkshake. But now, when things were much worse than that, she was smiling like everything was perfect, not hearing a word I said.

I turned and headed into the house, needing some ABBA to wipe away every last trace of this conversation.

• • •

The next day—the day of Dylan's demonstration—I dressed carefully, in a tight black anarchy T-shirt with matching black leggings, shooting for the perfect blend of political activist and sexy date.

After school I walked over to the Food Wagon, where Dylan was marching out front, a lone figure holding a huge sign that said FREEDOM AND JUSTICE FOR FOOD WAGON NOW. The fact that he was the only person demonstrating did not seem to faze him—he was chanting, and cursing at anyone who crossed his picket line to enter the store. "You're supporting slave labor!" he shouted at an old lady in a pale pink pantsuit, who gripped her purse and practically sprinted into the store.

"Hey," I said as I walked up.

Dylan's face lit up. "Matisse, great to see you! I'm glad someone besides me cares about workers' rights around here. Want a sign?" He gestured to the pile of signs he'd made for the event.

I knew I'd feel ridiculous hoisting a sign and carrying it around as part of a two-person demonstration, but Dylan looked so good, with his sharp cheekbones and big blue eyes, that I grabbed a sign and fell in step behind him.

"It's sick what's happening here," he called back to me as we circled the space in front of the double doors. "No health insurance, minimum wage—who can live like that?"

"That's messed up," I agreed.

"And that's why we're changing it!" he shouted, and then began chanting: *"What do we want? Justice! When do we want it? Now!"*

I joined in, feeling foolish. I'd been to proper

demonstrations at home, protesting war and labor violations, and there was always a loud crowd. Here it was just the two of us yelling our heads off.

But the people at the Food Wagon *were* being taken advantage of, and it clearly meant a lot to Dylan, so it seemed worth a little public humiliation. What did I care what people here thought of me?

A few minutes later a green car drove up, and out of it came Hal and a conservatively dressed woman. Her hair was in a neat French twist and her face was artfully made up. I'd never have believed such a person could be related to Hal the Hick, but her features were identical to his. There was no mistaking that she was his mother. Her lips twitched when she saw me and Dylan marching in front of the store.

"The workers of the Food Wagon are being exploited!" Dylan shouted when he caught sight of them.

Hal's mother rolled her eyes and walked into the store, but Hal walked over to us, looking concerned.

 84

"Really?" he asked.

"Yes," Dylan told him, clearly thrilled someone was finally showing some interest in our protest. "No health insurance, and they're expected to live on minimum wage."

"Did you talk to Mr. Sanspa about it?"

"Who?"

"The guy who runs Food Wagon."

"Of course not!" Dylan's voice was withering. "I don't engage in dialogue with the oppressor. I just help give voice to the oppressed."

"Hm." Hal tugged at his overalls straps and glanced over at me. I looked away. "I'm going to go talk to him." He walked toward the store.

"You're part of the problem if you're not working for the solution!" Dylan called after him. "What a wimp," he said.

"Really." I actually thought it probably was a good idea to talk to the guy in charge, but I wasn't missing an opportunity to slam Hal. "He's such a loser."

"Totally." Dylan resumed the march, shaking his sign with new vigor, as though the talk with Hal had recharged him.

About ten minutes later my feet hurt and I was tired of chanting. Dylan knew only two chants, and they were getting old. Plus we hadn't succeeded in turning anyone away from shopping at the Food Wagon. People just looked at us skeptically or laughed, and went about their shopping. I was debating how to tell Dylan I was ready to move on to some other activity (ideally making out), when out came Hal with a portly man who had a thick gray mustache and a shiny bald head. He was glaring as he walked toward us.

"What is the meaning of this?" he demanded.

"Who are you?" Dylan's eyes narrowed and he leaned forward, his sign balanced on one shoulder.

"No, who are *you*, spreading these lies about my store?" Clearly this was a pissed-off Mr. Sanspa.

Hal stood behind him, kicking at a bottle cap on the pavement.

"These are facts, not lies," Dylan insisted. "There's no health insurance for workers, and you expect them to live off minimum wage."

Mr. Sanspa glowered at Dylan. "For the first three months this is true. But after their trial period all workers get a raise and are entitled to health insurance. And they have a union! If they have a problem, they will tell me themselves. They don't need some punk kid and his girl-friend telling lies about my store. Get out of here."

Dylan opened his mouth but couldn't seem to find anything to say.

"If you are not gone in two minutes, I'll call the police!" Mr. Sanspa yelled, waving his arms at us.

We hurriedly gathered up the signs and took off. Hal and his mother passed us in their car. We could see his mother laughing and Hal beside her with a look on his face that I couldn't read. Probably feeling smug.

"That damn guy," Dylan sputtered. "What a phony! I just bet they have a union. Bunch of lies he fed us." His voice was harsh but his face was flaming—not that I blamed him. We'd looked like complete fools.

I walked along beside him, clutching several signs. A splinter was working its way into the base of my thumb, and I was having trouble keeping up with Dylan, who was practically running.

"That guy's going down," he said.

Dylan talked big, but he'd sure beat it out of there when Mr. Sanspa mentioned the police. People I knew at home who protested for social justice were serious about it, and a few had even been arrested. Not to mention they did research and found true problems—it sounded to me like things at the Food Wagon were pretty standard for grocery store employment. I was starting to think that Dylan was a bit of a rebel without a cause. Or a clue.

The splinter kept poking into me, and finally I stopped, not sure where we were headed and not even sure I wanted to hang out with Dylan anymore.

"I need to go home," I told him.

He walked back to where I was standing, and the yummy scent of coffee and shampoo wafted over me. "Hey, Matisse," he said, my name sounding like cream. "I'm so sorry about that. I had no idea it would go that way, with that crazy guy. But seriously, you were amazing!"

Suddenly Dylan didn't seem like such an idiot anymore. He took the signs from me and set them down, along with the ones he'd been holding. Then he ran a finger down my cheek. "You're so pretty," he said softly.

I leaned toward him, ready for a hard-earned kiss, when a car rounded the corner with a loud gunning of the engine. "Hey, get a room!" some guy shouted as the car squealed past.

I jumped in surprise and Dylan cursed. "All right, I'll let you get home. See you soon," he said.

Now that we were finally on the same wavelength, I was ready to hang out. But Dylan was picking up his signs, and I didn't want to seem too eager.

"See you," I said. As I headed home, I could still feel his fingers on my face, a promise of what was to come.

Chapter Seven

A loud, shrill sound woke me up just as the sun was rising on Friday morning. At first I thought it was a fire alarm, but it stopped and started irregularly. I couldn't figure out what it was and I couldn't get back to sleep. It was grating and persistent, and I finally just got up and dragged myself into the shower, feeling completely exhausted.

The early-morning light was gray and gloomy as I walked into the kitchen. And there at the table sat my dad. These days he was never out of bed when I left for school. In fact he was often in bed when I got home. But obviously the sound had woken him as well.

"I started coffee," he said, gesturing toward our jumbo-size coffeemaker.

"Great," I said. "Want some toast?"

"That sounds good. There's a raisin pumpernickel loaf in the Zabar's box."

A few days ago my mom had decided she couldn't live without Zabar's rugelach and placed an online order to the world's best food emporium—located, of course, in New York City. Yesterday the box had arrived overflowing with cheese, bread, coffee, and four kinds of rugelach.

"Perfect," I said.

I sliced up the loaf and popped the slices into the toaster, with the cozy sound of dripping coffee in the background.

"I've sure missed Zabar's," my dad said. "You can't find decent bread anywhere in this town."

"I know," I said. "All the bagels are like low-quality dinner rolls."

My dad laughed, a sound I hadn't heard in ages. "It's impossible to get good bagels anywhere besides New York."

The toaster pinged, and I grabbed two plates out of the cabinet, then passed one to my dad. I thought he had it in his hand, but as I let go, I realized that his fingers were moving in slow motion and they didn't have a firm grip. The plate balanced on his fingers for a moment, then crashed to the floor.

"Don't worry, Dad, these plates are kind of slippery," I said, cringing at how silly that sounded.

I tossed the shards in the garbage, then got out a new plate. But when I turned to give it to my dad, he was shuffling slowly out of the kitchen.

• • •

I could feel the beginning of a headache tapping at my temples as I closed the front door behind me. It had seemed like the morning couldn't get any worse, but as I walked across the porch, I saw Hal standing outside the house next door. I strode down the steps, looking ahead fiercely. He had to pick up on the fact that I'd rather get mowed down by a truck than talk to him.

"Hey, Matisse."

Or not. I sighed as loudly as I could, then looked over at Hal. "Hi." My voice was flat.

"Hey," he said again, needlessly, as he jumped off his porch and caught up with me. "I hope my rooster didn't bother you this morning."

"Your what? No, I don't think so." I kept my eyes ahead and my pace fast.

"Good—I was worried. He was crowing, and my mom—"

"Wait, he was *crowing*? Was that the god-awful sound at the crack of dawn? Kind of like a fire alarm?"

"Um, yeah, I guess."

I turned to glare at Hal. "So it's your fault I got woken up before the sun and feel like crap today?"

"Yeah, sorry. I was hoping he wouldn't bother anyone—my mom said if he bothered the neighbors, I'd have to get rid of him. And then my chickens will be depressed."

"Start the water for chicken soup, because he sure as hell did bother me." I was only half joking.

Hal was silent as we crossed Main Street

and turned left toward school. A quick glance in his direction revealed that his mouth was turned down and his eyes were sad. Then he took a deep breath.

"The thing is, I need this rooster. He's the start of my own farm. See, I really want to be a farmer, even though my folks think I'm crazy, and I want to start learning how to care for chickens now. And you need a rooster for chickens."

I could see how much the stupid rooster meant to him, and despite myself, I started to feel bad. "I'm just kidding about the soup. I'll get used to the crowing eventually."

Hal turned toward me, his whole face lit up. "Thanks for being a good sport."

I nodded, hoping that would be the end of it. But somehow he took my silence as an invitation to go on.

"I want to start an organic farm, with free-range chickens. I'm working after school for Farmer Delton and he's teaching me a lot, even though his farm isn't organic. But to me, organic farming makes the most sense. It's much more in tune with the universe, much more Zen, you know?"

I shook my head. "I don't really know anything about farming or Zen." Actually I did know something about it, because I'd studied Zen Buddhism at Friends. And to be honest, I was kind of impressed Hal was so up on it. But I certainly wasn't interested in talking to him about it. The last thing I needed was Hal thinking we were friends.

"It's all about living in rhythm with things, being in the moment but also staying detached." Hal turned to look at me, his eyes intense. "It's about finding meaning in the present, and letting go of control."

"Great," I said, picking up my pace and walking into school.

The girl from the pep rally, the one who'd had her arm around Hal, was skipping over, and he stopped to wait for her. She was surprisingly pretty—petite like a pixie, with long, thick black hair and big blue eyes.

"See you later, Matisse," Hal called as I headed down the hall.

"See you later," I replied automatically.

When I realized what I'd said, I could have kicked myself, because he was the last person I wanted to see later.

• • •

At lunch I told Violet the rooster story and Hal's stupid future plans. After the pep rally I'd worried that Violet might be mad at me, but she acted like it had never happened. And ever since then we'd stuck to safe topics, like Dylan and snarking on Prague. "Hal's such a moron," I concluded, pulling out my sandwich. It was on focaccia from the Zabar's box, with French brie and sliced avocado.

"I don't know. Organic farming is kind of cool. And at least Hal actually reads something." Violet was mixing a raspberry yogurt.

It irritated me how she always stuck up for him, so I changed the topic. "How's Mr. Milo High these days?" I asked. I bit into my sandwich and felt a pang of disappointment—my mom had ordered the wrong kind of brie.

Violet grimaced. "Even more of a jerk than usual. His mom told mine that I was at the pep rally, and now my mom's all psyched that maybe I'm turning into prom queen material."

"Why would he even talk to his mother about it?"

"Because he knows that she'll tell my mom and then my mom will start giving me a hard time. He loves to make my life hell." Violet glared across the cafeteria at Marco, who was sitting at the center table with Jennifer and several of the look-alike cheerleaders. A shaft of sunlight sparkled across their table, bathing them all in a golden glow, as though the universe was confirming their status.

"Him and his Satan's-spawn girlfriend."

"Well, you must be talking about the fabulous Jennifer!" Dylan's deep voice cut into our conversation—a welcome interruption. "Hey," I said eagerly.

He turned a chair around, then sat down and folded his arms across the back. "Hey, Matisse," he said softly. I felt a cozy warmth in my chest. "Hi, Violet," he added.

"Hey, Dylan," she said, twisting the top back onto her water bottle. "I've got to return a book at the library. See you guys later." She stood up and headed out of the cafeteria. I noticed that she took the long way around to avoid passing the golden table.

"So, Matisse," Dylan said. "What's new with you?"

"In this town is there ever anything new?"

Dylan laughed. "Good point." He reached out and began to stroke my arm with his finger-tips, creating delicious chills down my spine. "So I'm doing a big letter-writing campaign for Amnesty International tomorrow at my house, and I wondered if you wanted to come over and help out."

I was wary of Dylan's political actions after the fiasco at Food Wagon, but Amnesty International was a really solid organization, and I had written in letter campaigns at Friends.

"Definitely." It was a little disappointing that he wasn't asking me on a date yet, but I'd take what I could get.

"Great! It'll be you and me, and we can hang out afterward."

So it was a date! Of sorts.

"Come around two. I live on South Cape Road, number 243, the hideous white-and-green McMansion." He stood up and flipped the chair back so it was facing the right way again.

"Cool—I'll see you then." I watched him walk out.

• • •

That night I was practically singing when my mom called me down for dinner. I heard the TV as I passed my parents' bedroom, which meant the meal was just me and my mom, something that was happening pretty much all the time now. But I wasn't going to think about that, not when I had a date to focus on.

I sat down and took a slice of the spinach-and-feta quiche she'd made. "This looks great," I told her, spearing a big bite.

"Thanks. I was hoping you'd like it. I'm testing this recipe out for the party."

My fork froze halfway to my mouth. "What?"

"The party, for Dad's birthday."

"Yeah, I know what you meant. I just can't

believe you're still planning to do that."

"Of course I'm still planning it." She cut fiercely into her quiche.

"It's an awful idea. Everyone will hate it." I slammed my fork down.

"I don't know what you're talking about. It's going to be fun."

Her lips pursed so tightly, they were practically turning blue.

"Whatever," I said. I picked up my plate and walked into the kitchen, where I dumped the uneaten quiche in the garbage.

I stalked up the stairs toward my room, but as I passed the door to the stairs up to her studio, I slowed down. I'd been so caught up in school things lately that I'd been able to forget how it had looked when I was up there. But as I stared at the door, I remembered the eerie blank canvas. I felt icy prickles up and down my body.

I hesitated, then tiptoed over to the door and opened it. I slipped silently up the stairs, though my dad had the TV blaring, so it wasn't likely she'd hear me. And even if she did know I was going up there, her studio was never off-limits.

But I didn't want her to know how worried I was about her not painting. And maybe if I saw some evidence that she'd at least been sketching, I'd know that even though she was acting insane, she wasn't totally losing it.

But when I flipped on the light, I could see that nothing had changed since I'd last been there, weeks ago. I ran my hand over a thin layer of dust next to the sink. The room felt abandoned, as empty as the blank canvas staring at me. The tight feeling in my chest was threatening to cut off my breathing.

I turned off the light and fled down the stairs. As soon as I reached the safety of my room, I picked up my cell phone to call Violet. My hands were shaking, but I punched in the numbers, needing to hear her voice so I could focus all my attention on Dylan, instead of the fact that my mom just might be losing her mind.

• • •

On Saturday I had a long shower and took some extra time blow-drying my hair. Helping Amnesty International end torture was great, but making out was my priority for the day. I slid my feet into platform flip-flops and threw open the door to my room. I was ready.

I walked down the hall, and just as I passed my parents' bedroom, the door opened. It was my dad. He paused and then almost lurched out of the room. His feet moved as though they were cement blocks, and his arms were stiff at his sides. As he took another step, he tipped to the side and almost fell.

I felt my heart start to pound.

"Hey, Dad."

"Hi," he said gruffly.

"I have a date now," I said, just to say something. But then I realized it was a good thing to say.

There were dads who hated for their daughters to go out with guys, but my dad wasn't one of them. He'd always hang out while I was waiting for a date to show, pretending to be strict but really just kidding around. And when the night was over, more often than not I'd come home to the smell of fresh cocoa made from scratch. As soon as he heard me come in, he'd start whipping cream, the liquid slowly turning into rich fluff. We'd spoon gobs of it into our mugs and I'd tell him the PG version of my date. He'd give me advice, but mostly we'd kid around, just the two of us.

"It's with this guy Dylan," I said. "You'd love him." Which was my dad's cue to say he'd hate him.

"That's nice," he said vaguely.

My chest suddenly felt hollow. "He reminds me of Jordan," I said, naming one of the guys my dad had mocked endlessly.

"Well, have fun," he said. He was gazing past me, like I was already gone.

"Yeah, okay, see you later," I said.

I slipped past him and rushed out the door.

• • •

I tore up the road between my house and Dylan's. I needed to get out of there, and I needed to forget how my dad looked, gazing across the hall like I didn't exist. A major make-out session with Dylan was the only thing that could make that go away. And it was going to happen today, no matter what.

I took a wrong turn and ended up near the

farm with Satan's goose, but finally made my way to 243 South Cape Road. And it was truly a McMansion. It had three stories, about fifty sets of bay windows, these phony-looking white pillars, and a slick prefab look. The lawn had an overmanicured flower garden and carefully placed shrubs. Parked outside the double garage were a Mercedes convertible and a Saab. Dylan's parents had money and clearly wanted to show it.

I rang the bell, and after a few moments a snooty-looking girl answered. She was about twelve, with Dylan's blue eyes and thick black hair. She managed to stare down her nose at me even though she was a good six inches shorter. "Yes?" she asked, raising an eyebrow.

"I'm here for Dylan." I raised an eyebrow back.

"Who? Oh, you mean Cranston. Come on in. I think he's upstairs."

Cranston? I remembered that Violet had said Dylan wasn't his real name, but I'd had no idea his real name was so geeky.

After a minute Dylan appeared at the head of

the wide staircase leading to the upper floors.

"Matisse, come on up."

I trotted up the stairs, my hand running along the smooth wooden banister. I caught a glimpse of the huge living room, with one wall taken up by a fireplace. Portraits hung in the hall where Dylan was waiting for me.

"Are these people your relatives?" I asked, gesturing to them.

"Yeah, they're the family—a bunch of crooks, really. That's my great-grandfather—he bought the two farms where my family exploits migrant workers to this very day."

"Cranston, really." A tall, alarmingly thin woman had appeared in front of us. She was wearing a sleek dress and high heels and her face was expertly made up. No one else in Prague dressed like this.

"Mom, it's Dylan," he snapped, the whine in his voice making him sound like a two-year-old.

His mother sniffed. "You should be proud of your family name as well as your family's business." She turned to me.

"I'm Mrs. Browning," she said, holding out

her hand and gazing at me coolly.

"Matisse Osgood," I replied, giving her hand a hearty shake.

Her eyes ran over me, lips pursing at the sight of my Magenta Magic Moments lip gloss and deepening to a scowl when she saw all the skin between my tiny T-shirt and low-rise pants. "And where are you from, dear?" she asked. Her eyes told me that she thought I'd recently arrived from a big pile of trash.

"Manhattan, the Upper West Side," I said coolly.

"Really?" she asked, a smile tugging the corners of her mouth up—not too far, though. This was not a mouth to give in to a full-fledged smile. "Well, my goodness, I just love the city, all the art and the exquisite restaurants. We do have some lovely culture here, but it must seem very rustic to you."

"Yup."

Dylan cackled.

"See you, Mom. We're writing letters for Amnesty International," he said, turning and leading me down the long hall.

"Lovely to meet you, Matisse," she called after us.

At the end of the hall he opened a door to a large room with bay windows overlooking an Olympic-size pool in the backyard. The snooty sister was curled in a deck chair next to the pool, wearing a big sweatshirt and watching a portable DVD player.

"Have a seat," Dylan said, gesturing to the sofa along one wall of the room. He settled into a love seat across from the sofa. A wide glass coffee table separated the two. Bob Dylan posters covered the walls, and a stereo was pumping Bob Marley. A desk in the corner held a laptop computer and a pile of CD cases. Dylan's unmade bed was under the windows. It looked like a small apartment.

I glanced at the sofa, then settled on the love seat next to Dylan.

"So," he began, riffling though a folder on the coffee table. "I printed out the campaign info last night. I figured we could make some notes and then type up a bunch of letters. It's better if you write your own instead of just copying the ones they do." A lock of his hair fell into his eyes as he bent over the papers.

I moved closer to him and smoothed the lock back into place. He glanced over at me and smiled.

"Why don't you start with these?" He tossed a pile of papers on my lap.

Damn.

I shifted my weight and the papers began to slide. We both grabbed for them.

"Be careful—they're in order," he said, then settled down to read.

Obviously it was work before play. I looked down at the top page in my lap, but the words didn't gel into coherent sentences. Instead all I could see was my dad's vacant stare. His empty voice echoed in my head.

I looked up at Dylan, whose face was scrunched in concentration. He was into it, but too bad. I needed to get my dad out of my head. I set the papers on the coffee table and slid across the love seat so that my leg was up against his. Then I grabbed the rest of the papers out of his lap and tossed them on the table as well. He reached for them, but I took his hand, lacing my fingers together with his. "There's no rush," I murmured, leaning toward him. With my free hand I ran my fingers down the side of his face.

He took a last glance at the papers, then put his arms around me and pulled me close. I snuggled in and lifted my face to his. The first kiss was a little awkward—it hit on my cheek and then he came in too hard and our teeth bumped. But after that we got it, his lips soft on mine, his tongue exploring my mouth. Okay, exploring a little too zealously, but it wasn't a bad start. I pressed my body against his, kissing him a little harder. He tangled a hand in my hair, pulling me in tighter.

This was what I'd been longing for, to get lost, let my mind go and my body take over. But somehow it wasn't happening. My mind was in overdrive, making me hyper aware of where Dylan was pulling too hard on my hair and how his teeth kept hitting my lip. This wasn't the escape I'd come for. The longer it went, the worse I felt.

Finally Dylan pulled back and gave me a slow smile. "That was nice," he said in what he obviously thought was a sexy voice. "Let's get to work, and we can take another break soon."

He handed me my pile of papers and I stared at them blankly. In my head my dad's voice rang louder than ever. And I knew that no amount of making out was going to quiet it. In fact, I was starting to wonder if anything could. I suddenly missed my dad so much that it felt like my chest had been ripped open.

"You know, I think I'll head out," I said as evenly as I could.

"But we didn't even start writing letters yet," Dylan whined.

"I'm sorry," I said.

"I really question your commitment to social issues, Matisse," Dylan said solemnly as he followed me out of the room.

"Yeah, I think you're onto something there. I may not be a true revolutionary."

"If you're not part of the solution, you're part of the problem," he said in a snide voice.

"Right now I think I can live with that," I

said as I ran down the stairs.

"You're letting down torture victims all over the world!" he shouted as I threw open the front door.

At some point I did want to be able to help torture victims. But first I needed to figure out how to help myself.

• • •

Violet called that night as I was surfing the web trying to find a new form of distraction.

"How was it?" she asked eagerly.

"What?"

"Your big date with Dylan!"

"Oh, yeah, that. It was a total bust. All he's interested in is someone to do political stuff with."

"Disappointing," she said.

"Yeah. And his real name is Cranston."

Violet gasped. "That's wretched!"

"Yeah, totally."

"I'm sorry it sucked," she said. "You sound pretty disappointed."

I was hit with the surprising notion that right at this moment it would feel amazing to tell her about my dad. But then I thought about what would happen next week, when she asked me about it, when all I'd want to do was forget it was happening.

"Guys are weird," I said. "What're you doing tonight?"

Chapter Eight

On Sunday I holed up in my room and hoped my mom would forget about my company at dinner. But of course that was like hoping I'd wake up one morning in our condo in the city, with the sounds of traffic outside my window. So when she called me down just after six o'clock, I faced the inevitable and went.

The sun was setting earlier now, so my mom had turned on the ugly fluorescent overhead. She had said she'd get a new light for the kitchen, but so far it hadn't happened. We sat across from each other, the sharp light too bright. When I looked at my mom, I noticed that her hair was in desperate need of a trim and the dark circles under her eyes seemed permanent. She'd lost weight and her face looked almost gaunt. For the first time, I could see how Hal might mistake her for my grandmother.

While my mom prattled on about how much she loved her garden, I stayed silent, wolfing down the chunks of tomato and eggplant so that I could escape back up to my room. I made sure to nod and smile so she'd think I was listening. But then something she said caught my attention.

"So they'll be here around eight," she said, and then took a large bite of salad.

"Wait, what? Who's coming where?"

Her brow furrowed. "I just told you," she said after she'd swallowed. "The Millers are coming to buy a painting from me. They're choosing between *Desert Sky* and *Sally in the Morning*."

Why did the name Miller sound familiar? "Who are they?"

"A family here. I met her at the grocery store—she recognized me from that article in the *Prague Post* and she wanted to buy something. I think she said it would be for her daughter."

"I thought you were using *Sally* in your spring show."

"Oh, well, it's no problem if they take it. I can use something else."

"Right, of course," I said. I realized that maybe if she sold something, it would spark her interest in painting. If she started painting again, I knew she'd be okay. "That's awesome you have a sale."

"Thanks." Her voice was laced with pleasure. "They'll be here at eight, and I think you should come say hi. They have a daughter around your age."

I nodded. Miller. Why did I know that name?

• • •

I was in my room when the doorbell rang. "They're here!" my mom called to me as she went to answer it. I headed downstairs, gathering my energy to be friendly. But as I walked into the living room, it was all I could do not to gasp.

Jennifer was in my home.

She stood between her parents, who were smiling phony smiles at my mother. Her mom was a pale blond with a big nose and squinty eyes. Her dad was going bald and had a fat belly. It was difficult to understand how they had produced the modelesque Jennifer, with her perfect, even features and sparkling blond hair.

"Matt, Claire, Jennifer, I'd like you to meet my daughter, Matisse," my mom said as I walked into the room.

"How sweet, you named her after an artist," Claire simpered.

Matt nodded at me, and Jennifer's eyes were two rays of undiluted hatred.

"And this is our Jennifer," Claire said, placing a hand on Jennifer's shoulder. "Do you girls know each other from school?"

Neither of us answered—we were too busy staring each other down.

"Jennifer is a cheerleader," Claire told me proudly, smoothing Jennifer's hair.

Jennifer shook her mom's hand off.

"Well, how about we leave the kids down

here and I'll show you the paintings," my mom said quickly. She knew how I felt about cheer-leading.

"I want to see the paintings too," Jennifer announced.

Claire beamed, and the whole toxic family walked toward the studio in the attic.

I flopped onto the sofa, feeling helpless and furious, and took a mental inventory of the back of the house: the two bedrooms, the bathroom, the guest room. The worst that could happen was that she would hear some cheesy TV show that my dad was watching, but that wasn't so bad, was it? He always kept the door closed— he didn't want his own family to see him lying there, let alone a bunch of strangers. And even if my mom did have some PD books or info lying around, there was no reason for them to connect it to my dad. I was probably safe.

But deep down I knew I'd never feel safe around Jennifer again. She knew where I lived, she had probably noticed the family pictures in the living room, so she'd know my dad if he ever ventured out of the house. And then what if he did go out and an off period hit, like that time I saw him in the bookstore?

I heard my mom laugh from the attic and I realized this whole thing was her fault. How dare she bring Jennifer into our house!

I heard a door close, and a few minutes later they all came trooping in.

"It's just gorgeous," Claire was saying. "I don't really know a lot about art, but I can tell this is something special."

It was all I could do not to gag.

My mom was smiling and even silent Matt looked pleased. Jennifer had a small smile on her face, and when she saw me she gave me a strange look, almost triumphant. I just glared at her. She probably hated my mom's art, which was not unexpected: I doubted anyone here could truly appreciate my mom's stuff, which was very stark and abstract.

"I'll get it to you next week," my mom said.

"We just can't wait!" Claire replied, and with a few more compliments, the Millers finally left.

"Well, that went well," my mom said, walking into the living room.

"How could you do that? How could you invite them here?" I shouted.

Her face fell. "What do you mean? I thought they were nice."

I suppressed a scream at the thought of anyone ever calling Jennifer nice. "Mom, that girl is evil."

"Honey, I know you don't like cheerleading, but it seems a bit harsh to call her evil."

"It's not harsh, it's an understatement!"

My mom rubbed her forehead. "I'm sorry you don't like her, but—"

"You mean you're sorry I hate her," I said.

"The point is that this is where my studio is—clients have to come here to buy paintings."

I knew she was right and it wasn't like she could undo what had happened, so I headed upstairs to put on some ABBA to wipe out all thoughts of Jennifer's presence in my home.

• • •

The next day I woke up late, probably because of the Jennifer nightmares I'd had all night long. I took a superfast shower and ran half of the way to school. I was huffing and puffing as I staggered through the main doors of the school.

As I started down the main hall, something weird happened. Usually people ignored me, but today they were glancing at me and poking each other as I walked by. Instead of the usual loud shrieks, their voices lowered as I passed. Even Sherry was quiet, and I caught her staring at me as I shoved my bag into my locker.

"What?" I asked her.

"Oh, nothing." Her voice was squeaky. She shut her locker quickly and walked down the hall, whispering with her friends. One glanced back at me, and when she met my eyes, she jerked her head around so fast that I was worried she'd hurt herself.

It continued as I walked to class. I was starting to feel like everyone in the school was talking about me. Between the whispers when I passed, the stares that never quite met my eyes, and the way even my teachers looked at me strangely, I was began to feel very uneasy. In third period the little phone on the wall of the classroom rang. Mr. Garner jumped a mile, making us all laugh, and when he picked it up he spoke gruffly, as though trying to reclaim his dignity.

"Matisse Osgood?" His eyes found me slouched in the last row. "Yes, she's here. To the counselor now? Fine." He hung up. "Matisse, you need to go to the school counselor's office," he told me, as though the entire class hadn't already heard.

I was confused and annoyed, and actually felt my cheeks get hot when everyone in the class turned to stare at me as I walked out. What the hell was going on?

I left the classroom and made my way to the counselor's office, where she was waiting for me outside the door. She ushered me in, looking very solemn. I plunked myself down in the hard wooden chair that was the only seat in the place besides hers. Posters with uplifting slogans hung on the wall, and I stared at one of a kitten climbing a tree. It said *You can make it if you just put your mind to it*. The kitten probably got to the top and then cried until a fireman came and took him down to safety.

"Matisse, hi, I'm Miss Bertram," she began,

her watery green eyes magnified by thick tortoiseshell glasses. Hadn't she heard that no one used *Miss* anymore? "My job is to help students, to be someone you can really talk to about what's going on." She spread out her hands like she was bearer of the earth's bounty. "I'm here to listen."

I stayed silent.

"I know things can be hard. Maybe there are some things happening at home that you'd like to talk about," she said softly.

Damn! My body slumped in the chair. Jennifer must have somehow found out about my dad and now the whole stupid school knew, including this pathetic windbag in front of me. This sucked.

I pulled myself up and fixed my gaze on Miss Bertram. "I can assure you there's nothing I need to talk about with you." My voice was firm.

"Well, I just . . ." She fumbled, tugging on a strand of her gray hair. "Here, let me just give you this"—she picked up a pamphlet—"and you can look it over in your free time. Know that I'm here if you need me."

The day I needed her was the day I'd hang myself. I stood up and she leaned over, pressing the pamphlet into my hand.

I pulled her office door open so hard it hurt my arm, and I flew out of there as fast as I could. There was no way I was going back to class now. I headed to the bathroom and locked myself in a stall, where I leaned my back against the door and took deep breaths. There was no need to lose it—this wasn't going to break me.

My heart rate calmed, and I realized that the stupid pamphlet Miss Bertram had given me was still clutched in my hand. I glanced at it, ready for more kittens with clichés, or worse, something about PD. But the words on the cover took me by surprise: SUPPORT FOR FAMILIES OF ADDICTS it said in bright red letters.

What?

• • •

Violet wasn't in the cafeteria when I got there. I tapped my fingers on the table and tried to ignore the furtive looks so many people were sending my way. But even when I couldn't see them, I could feel them, like prodding little stabs in my back.

Finally I saw Violet carrying her tray over to our table. It was like someone had tossed me a life raft as I was drowning in an ocean of weirdness.

She sat down. "Hey." She picked up the plastic packet holding her fork and focused all her attention on opening it.

"Violet, what the hell's going on here?" I exploded, causing several people at nearby tables to look over. I didn't even have it in me to stare them down. "Why am I suddenly the freak of Milo High?"

"It's about your family." Violet's voice was chilly. "Your dad. I guess Jennifer was over last night with her parents, and she saw when she went to the bathroom."

What could Jennifer have seen in the bathroom? It wasn't like my dad was hanging out there. "What do you mean?"

"Well, like, all the pills. She looked in the medicine cabinet and she saw all the bottles." Violet poked savagely at her mashed potatoes. "You could have told me your dad had an addiction, you know. I may be from Prague, but I'm not a total hick. I know about drug problems."

"Wait, so Jennifer saw all the medicine and thought my dad was some kind of drug addict?"

"Yeah, addicted to prescription pills," Violet said.

Well, that explained the pamphlet from the counselor. And all the looks—this was probably the biggest scandal ever to hit Milo High, a girl with an addict for a dad. It figured that Jennifer spied in our medicine cabinet, then didn't understand any of the meds and just jumped to the most sensational thing she could.

I focused back in on Violet, who was shoving bites of meat loaf into her mouth and not saying anything. My stomach felt like the inside of a washing machine.

"Violet . . ." I began, having no idea where I was going.

"Hey, Violet. Hey, Matisse."

I turned my head to see who was brave enough to be seen speaking to me in public and was surprised to find myself staring into Hal's hazel eyes.

"What's up?" Violet said, her voice friendly for Hal.

"Just wanted to see how Matisse was doing," Hal said, pulling out a chair and sitting down. "Being the latest story in the Milo High gossip mill is never fun."

"Tell me about it." We all looked up as Marco walked over. He leaned in and rested his palms on the table.

Violet's eyes narrowed. "Here to find out all the dirt?" she asked him.

"Relax. I just came to see how Matisse was doing," Marco said. "No one's on a spying mission."

Violet snorted. "Right."

"I'm fine," I said. I was surprised he'd come over, and I was pretty sure he wasn't there to spy. Marco didn't strike me as a gossipmonger.

"Good," Marco said. "Whatever's going on in your family is your business; but as you've probably already noticed, the Milo gossip mill is famous for getting the story wrong." He turned to Hal and Violet. "Remember the time some jerk started a rumor that I was part of a gambling ring and trying to throw games?"

Hal laughed. "There were even rumors that

the new secretary in the office was really working for the FBI on a sting operation."

Violet's forehead was creased, but she didn't say anything.

"So don't be surprised if you start hearing all kinds of things about your life that you had no idea about," Marco said to me.

"Yeah, accuracy isn't exactly top priority." Hal put his hand on my arm. "Matisse, I don't know what the deal is with your dad, but let me know if you ever need to get out of the house or anything."

Marco was nodding.

I felt my face heat up. I couldn't let them keep thinking the wrong thing about my dad. But the thought of trying to tell them anything close to the truth made me feel like I might pass out.

"Um, my dad isn't an addict," I finally blurted out. My face was on fire.

"You don't have to tell us anything," Hal said. "It's your business, no one else's." His hand was still on my arm, and its warmth was comforting.

"Marco!" Jennifer's shriek carried across the cafeteria, making me jump.

"I've got something to take care of," Marco said, standing up. "Hang in there, Matisse. Someone will cheat on a test or get suspended for smoking and you'll be old news." He walked off to meet Jennifer.

"He acts all supportive, but then he goes off with the one who started all this," Violet said.

"Maybe he doesn't know it was her." Hal pushed his chair back and stood up. "But he's right, Matisse, this will blow over."

I nodded, feeling a little wobbly. I'd never have expected Hal and Marco to be so great to me.

"See you guys," he said.

"He's nice," Violet said. She bit her thumbnail for a second, then took a deep breath. "Nicer than me. I shouldn't have just assumed Jennifer was telling the truth about your dad. I'm sorry."

"Oh, don't worry about it," I said, feeling a sweet prick of relief that she wasn't mad anymore.

"And Hal was right—you don't have to explain anything. But I'm here if you ever want to talk."

"Thanks." I had trouble getting the word out, because of course Violet had every right to ask me about it and I knew that she deserved the truth. But the truth was stuck somewhere low in my gut and there was no way I could get it out. So I picked up my rugelach and took a bite.

Violet began telling me about the latest story she was working on for the magazine. She was trying to distract me, to make me feel better. The rugelach felt like a clump of wet dust in my mouth, and I finally had to spit it out in my napkin.

• • •

When I walked in through the front door of my house, all I wanted to do was collapse into bed. I crossed my fingers and hoped that my mother was out, and for once my wish was granted— I found a note on the kitchen table reminding me that my parents were in the city for my dad's monthly appointment with the Genius. With everything that had happened, I'd totally forgotten the appointment.

I walked to my room, wriggled out of my jeans—which felt like tight cardboard around my legs—threw on my old terry cloth robe, and lay down on my bed. I had something new to worry about now: right before we moved, Ceese got my mom to tell her my dad's appointment schedule with the Genius. She made all these plans for us to cut school and hang out together in the city on those days. I didn't have the heart to tell her then that there was no chance in hell I'd ever willingly get into a car to take my dad to see the Genius—he was at his darkest before those appointments. And I hadn't said anything about it to her recently, either. She probably thought I was still coming.

The phone rang and I waited till it stopped, then hopped off the bed and switched off my cell and the ringer on the hall phone. There was certainly no one I wanted to talk to now. Back in my room I slipped into bed, snuggled under the covers, and fell into a heavy sleep.

Voices in the hall outside my room woke me up. My mouth felt linty, and my head pounded when I lifted it off my pillow. Outside, it was dark, and I wondered how long I'd been sleeping. Clearly awhile, if my parents were already home. I pulled myself up and stretched. My stomach growled and I decided to go heat up one of the frozen veggie burritos we had stockpiled in the freezer. I padded barefoot to the door.

"Don, what are you doing?" My mom's voice stopped me. It didn't sound quite right.

I heard my dad mumble something. Then their bedroom door slammed.

"Don't you walk away from me!" I heard the door handle rattle. "Unlock the door this minute." More rattling.

My heart started to pound, hard and heavy in my chest.

"You can't lock me out of my own bedroom!" She was yelling now. "Let me in!"

Silence from my dad.

"Please don't shut me out, Blue! We need to talk, to go through this together!" Her screams had a hysterical edge.

My legs could no longer hold me up. I slid

down to the floor, my head leaning against the wall.

"I'm not living like this anymore!" I heard her fists pounding on the door. "Let me in now!"

We both waited, but the door didn't open.

"I hate this!" she shouted. "I hate my life, I hate this disease, and I hate you!" Her voice broke on the last word and she began to sob, a sound so wild and ugly it hurt.

My hands were slick with sweat, and my heart was beating so hard, it felt like it could rip out of my chest.

I knew I couldn't do this anymore either.

Chapter Nine

Violet was sitting at our usual table when I walked into the cafeteria the next day. I took a deep breath and headed over to her. "My dad has Parkinson's disease," I said in a rush. "That's why there's all that medicine in the bathroom." Sweat was prickling my temples and palms. "And everyone in my family has been pretending it isn't happening. Including me. That's why I never talked about it." I pulled out a chair and collapsed into it.

Violet's eyes were wide. "Oh, my God! I can't believe I listened to Jennifer." Her eyes were filled with sympathy. "I'm so sorry, Matisse."

"Yeah." My voice was gravelly. I cleared my throat. "It's okay." The gravel was still there.

"How long has he had it?" she asked.

"Well, he was diagnosed like five years ago, but it didn't get really bad until last year." I felt naked talking about it.

"Oh, is that why you guys moved here?" Violet asked, her voice tentative.

"Yeah, pretty much. My dad couldn't sculpt anymore, so he didn't want to be in the city."

"Wow, that sucks," she said, pulling on a curl. "I had no idea."

I made a small noise that was almost a laugh. "It's not like I've been into discussing it."

One corner of Violet's mouth curled up. "Yeah, you're not exactly an open book. But I can understand why. I'm sure it's been really hard."

I nodded, not trusting my voice.

"My grandpa had Alzheimer's, and it sucked. My mom totally freaked and cried every time it was mentioned." Violet's face was scrunched, like she wasn't sure her story was making me feel better or worse. "Not that that's how you act or anything. You know what I mean."

"Yeah, well, I guess we're all pretty freaked." I remembered the sounds of my mother's hysterical crying and felt my stomach twist. "How's your grandfather now?"

"Well, dead, actually." Violet looked like she'd accidentally swallowed a rotten apple. "Not such a comforting story. But he was old and all. I'm sure your dad, I mean, I . . ." She fumbled, her face now turning a shade of cranberry. "Actually, I don't mean anything. I don't know what Parkinson's even is; I just know it's what Michael J. Fox has and it makes you shake."

"Yeah, and your muscles can get all stiff. Meds help sometimes, for periods of time." I took a breath and clenched my hands. "Please don't say anything to anyone, okay? I can't take people asking me about it and being all sorry for me and stuff."

"Don't worry, I won't," Violet said solemnly.

I cleared my throat. "So Jennifer really has the school thinking my dad is an addict?"

135

"Yeah, pretty much."

"Well, let them think whatever they want."

"Maybe you could start a rumor that he parties with rock stars or something. People believe anything."

I tried to smile, but I was still feeling shaky from what I'd told Violet. "Just as long as they leave me the hell alone."

• • •

As I was walking to my last class of the day, I felt someone touch my back. I spun around, ready for anything.

It was Marco.

"Sorry, didn't mean to scare you," he said, looking serious. "Can I talk to you for a sec?"

I nodded, and he pulled me into an alcove.

"I didn't know it was Jennifer who spread that stuff about your dad, and when she told me, I dumped her. I don't know what the deal is with your dad, but she shouldn't have said anything."

He sauntered away, leaving me speechless as the late bell rang.

• • •

I took a long route home after school. So far I'd avoided seeing my mom, and I was hoping to keep it that way. I tiptoed up the porch steps and twisted the doorknob slowly, ready to sneak upstairs. But as soon as I opened the front door, there she was, sitting on the sofa waiting for me.

"Hey, sweetie. Take a seat—we need to talk." She patted a spot next to her on the sofa. She still had the dark circles under her eyes, but her gaze was clear. I slumped down next to her and stared at the leg of the glass coffee table.

"I'm sure you heard what happened last night, how I kind of lost it." Her voice was calm. "The thing is, I'm not sure we've been handling this right. Dad wanted us to go on like we've always been, and not let the PD take over our lives."

I noticed a nick on the table leg, just a tiny curve where a sliver of glass had been jarred loose.

"But that hasn't really worked." She took a deep breath. "It wasn't fair to any of us, to your dad, to me, or to you." I could feel her eyes on me, but I continued to stare at the sharp section of missing glass. "We need to start talking about this, honey. We need to start accepting it and dealing with it."

There was a pause. I guess I was supposed to start pouring out my heart. But just because my mom thought it was time to start talking didn't mean I felt like it.

"Whatever," I said, standing up.

"No, not *whatever*. We need to get things out in the open, start really dealing with all the changes." She reached out her hand to me. "Let's talk about how you're feeling."

"I'm feeling like I want you to leave me alone." My voice was brittle. I was on my way to my room before she could say anything else.

I sat down and opened a book and tried to read, but my vision was blurred. I jumped up and went over to my computer, trying to find some distraction. It was like every terrible, unthinkable feeling about my dad was trapped inside the wound inside me, raw and oozing underneath the thick layer of scar tissue. I could feel it pulsing, deep and dense. My mom's meltdown and now her pushing me to talk put pressure on the wound. I'd thought telling Violet would help, but it hadn't.

I knew I had to figure out some way to relieve the pressure.

• • •

Midweek I made the mistake of checking email, and there were six messages from Ceese, all pissed that I had stood her up when my parents went into the city. Well, I was sure that was what they said—I didn't actually bother to read them.

• • •

On Thursday as I was walking past Hal's house, I heard yelling. After a second the door flew open and Hal stomped out.

"I mean it, young man!" his mother yelled from inside the house.

"Yes, I know." I could hear in Hal's voice how hard he was straining not to yell back. If his parents actually called him "young man" when they were pissed, they were probably the kind of parents you couldn't yell at.

As Hal vaulted over the porch rail, I ducked behind one of the bushes lining his yard. I didn't want him to know I'd heard anything, but he took off in the other direction, never even looking my way. I straightened up, feeling a little silly for hiding, and walked up to my house.

Apparently we weren't the only family hiding some kind of mess behind closed doors. Though given how Norman Rockwell-ish Hal and his parents seemed, it was probably just that he'd forgotten to call his father "sir" or something.

• • •

That night my mom knocked on my door. I was at the computer, reading reviews of films that I would never see because Prague had no independent movie theater.

"What?"

"Dinner," her voice rang out.

"Not hungry." I clicked to read more reviews of a Russian movie about three friends committing suicide.

"Too bad. We're eating as a family now."

I paused—what the hell did that mean? "I'm really not hungry."

"Then come sit with me and Dad, and keep us company while we eat."

Keep her and *Dad* company? Since when was he doing family meals? After my mom's meltdown, he'd barely been out of the bedroom. And the three of us hadn't been in the same room together since then. Anxiety fluttered in my chest.

"I mean it, Matisse—we're eating family dinners from now on." She was using her serious voice now.

I shut off my computer and slouched down the stairs. My dad was already sitting at the table. His face was stiff but he was glaring at my mom, and I felt slightly better. Obviously I wasn't the only one put off by the enforced together time.

My mom bustled about, putting dishes of food on the table. She'd gone all out, making fajitas with six different vegetables, two kinds of shredded cheese, and homemade tortillas. When all the fixings were on the table, she pulled out her chair and sat down.

"Blue, I wasn't sure if you'd want to try to wrestle with a tortilla, but I figured you'd enjoy the rest. Go ahead, dig in," my mom said, reaching for the plate of tortillas and spreading one out on her plate. She passed the plate to me, then handed the broccoli to my dad. I set down the tortilla plate without taking any. My dad passed me broccoli without serving himself. I put it down without taking any either. Next came mushrooms, onions, cheese, and guacamole, my mother heaping them onto her plate, and my dad and I setting each down untouched.

My mother appeared not to notice. "This looks great!" She wrapped up her fajita. It was so big, the sides of the tortilla barely held together and a rogue piece of broccoli popped out as she took a huge bite. "Delish! So, Matisse, how was your day?"

"Fine."

"Anything interesting happen?"

"No." I toyed with my fork.

"Oh, that's right, nothing interesting ever happens to you at Milo High."

I caught myself before I laughed.

She turned to my dad. "Blue, how was your day?"

"Fabulous and riveting." My dad's voice was coated with hostility.

She clicked her tongue. "Right, okay. Well, if you guys want to be wet blankets, that's fine, I'll just tell you about my day. I started work on a new piece this morning."

I stopped glaring down at the table and looked at my mom in surprise.

"I haven't felt up to painting for a while now, but today I did. I think I was ready."

I poked my fork though a hole in my woven place mat to avoid her gaze. My cheeks felt hot and I held my breath. I heard my dad cough. If she started in on how we all needed to talk, I was out of there.

But her eyes took on a distant look, like she was away from the table and up in her studio, staring at the infant stages of her painting. "It's going to be all in shades of red and orange. I was driving by one of the orchards yesterday, and the apples against the fall leaves were just mesmerizing. I had to park the car and just look." Her voice was animated as she told us how the apple orchards in autumn were her muse for the new work.

I felt a momentary peacefulness wash over me as she went on. She hadn't sounded so excited in ages.

My mom finally took her last bite of fajita and wiped her mouth delicately with her napkin. "That was great. Why don't you guys clean up, since I did all the cooking."

I froze. The last thing in the world that I wanted was to be alone in the kitchen with my dad. What if I passed him something too fast and he broke it again? The meds seemed to be working, since he wasn't shaking or anything, but you never knew for sure. And even if they were working, I didn't want to be alone with him. It just felt too hard.

But when I turned to my mom to protest, I saw steel behind her smile. I stood up slowly and picked up the bowl of broccoli and my empty plate. I headed into the kitchen, where I packed the leftover broccoli in a plastic container and rinsed out the bowl for the dishwasher. I heard my dad walk in and set something on the counter. I kept my back turned, and only when he'd shuffled back to the table did I grab the bowls of peppers and onions he'd left.

He cleared, I put away leftovers and loaded the dishwasher, and my mom sat in the living room, smug as could be.

• • •

The next morning my mom caught me as I was pouring a cup of coffee.

Her hair was a mess and she was wearing her ugly pink flannel nightshirt, but for the first time in months her skin glowed and her eyes sparkled. And I noticed paint speckles on her hands.

The peaceful feeling from last night filled me again. I took a deep breath, appreciating the light atmosphere.

"Morning, hon," she said casually, as she grabbed a mug out of the cabinet.

"Morning," I said, more warmly than she deserved. It just felt so good to see her normal.

"Sweetie, I wanted to explain a little about last night. I feel bad about how I've handled things, pretending everything was fine. I'm not going to do that anymore, and I don't think any of us should. We need to start facing things together and stop pretending." She looked at me and smiled sadly. "Acceptance comes in stages. But I think we need to be realistic about Dad's future."

The lightness in the room evaporated and I felt hot and itchy, like my skin didn't fit right.

"When you're ready, we'll talk. I won't push, I promise."

I nodded, gulped down the rest of my coffee, and headed out. As I walked, I tried to focus on *A Tale of Two Cities*, which we'd just started in my English class, and when that didn't work, I started a mental inventory of my closet, to decide what new things I needed for winter. Anything not to think about what my mom had said. I was practically running to get to school, where Violet, my classes, and even Jennifer could distract me from the pain that was eating away at my insides.

Chapter Ten

On Monday morning I had just started off for school when I heard someone call my name. I knew it was Hal even before I turned around to see him in his usual overalls and a beat-up blue jacket, loping to catch up with me.

"What?" Why couldn't this guy take a hint? Yeah, he'd been really nice after Jennifer started the rumors about my dad, but that didn't mean I wanted him nosing around my house.

"I just wanted to walk to school with you." I saw hurt in his eyes and felt a surprising stab of guilt. This guy was the number-one person I needed to keep at a distance, but for some weird reason it made me feel bad to keep pushing him away.

"Okay, sure," I said, promising myself that I'd be better at ditching him the next time.

"Your mom is doing a great job with your yard—I saw she put in bulbs and everything."

He *would* start off a conversation with a winner like that. "You mean my grandma?" I meant it as a barb, but somehow it came out as playful.

His ears turned pink. "Sorry about that."

"No, I'm just giving you a hard time. A lot of people have kids later in the city." This nice thing was getting out of control, but I couldn't seem to stop.

"That's right, you're from New York."

"Yeah." I waited for him to gush over how cool that was.

He paused. "I think I'd find it hard not to have open fields and woods to wander around in," he said.

"I hate open fields and I'd rather shoot my foot off than go into the woods," I said conversationally.

Hal laughed. "Yeah, I kind of guessed that." His glance took in my glitter ballet slippers and pencil skirt. Not exactly hiking clothes. "So, how do you like Prague?"

We had reached the corner and waited while a lone car passed. The air was cold but the sun felt warm on my skin.

"I hate it."

"Seriously?"

"Pretty much. I just hate how little there is to do and how the people here are so narrow." First I was nice, now I was spilling my guts— there was seriously something wrong with me today.

He reached out his hand and brushed it along the row of bushes that lined the block we were walking on. "There's stuff to do here. Maybe not the Museum of Modern Art, but there's other cool stuff you might like."

"Like what?"

"Do you like to ski? We have great cross-country skiing in the winter. And skating on Heron's Pond."

"I never go out in the cold."

"Well, you can swim in the lake in the summer."

"I don't do lakes—fresh water has nasty stuff in it," I said.

"Okay, well, there are fun town activities, like the hayride and Pumpkin Fest. And there's Bird Day, where we all dress up like our favorite bird and run around town flapping our arms."

I almost choked. "What?"

"Gotcha! We're not that bad." He had a bit of a bounce in his step now.

I shook my head and fought back a smile. "Bird Day. You know, I believed you for a second. I think this place is capable of a Bird Day."

"Well, maybe we should start it. That's one of the cool things about a small town. You can organize events if you want. I'm kidding about us organizing a Bird Day, though—I'm not sure it would fly."

I groaned, but this time I couldn't hide the smile. Who'd have thought Hal was actually capable of making a pun?

We'd reached school, and as we started walking on the pathway leading up to the building,

Hal put a hand on my arm. His eyes were serious when I turned to face him.

"You have a point about people sometimes being a little narrow. I'm not sure if it's any better in the city, but here people really do like to gossip." His eyes flicked toward the school, then met mine again. "A lot of people are great, but some aren't, and I know they're making things tough for you right now. I brought you something that might help."

I was too surprised by his insight and thoughtfulness to form an intelligent response.

He pulled open his backpack, and for a brief second I expected him to take out a can of mace or a set of nunchucks. Instead he handed me a ratty paperback book with a mandala on the cover. "It's about meditation, how to do it and stuff. It might not be your thing, but give it a try. It's helped me out when I was totally stressed." He handed me the book, and I reached for it automatically.

The first bell rang.

"Let me know what you think," he said, jogging up the steps. "I'll see you later."

I walked slowly up the steps, ignoring the looks that came from all directions. As I walked down the hall, I tucked the book into my bag.

Hal was full of surprises.

• • •

At the end of the day I was in a bad mood. I'd thought the rumors would be dying down, but people were still staring at me all the time. I tugged at my locker, wishing someone would get caught having sex under the bleachers or smoking pot in the science lab so there'd be something new for the grapevine.

"Matisse?"

I turned, surprised to hear Violet's voice. "Hey, don't you have the magazine now?"

"Yeah, but I had to tell you something, something I just heard." Her face was somber.

I felt my whole body go stiff. Someone must have found out the truth about my dad. That was why I was getting so much more attention.

"Everyone is saying that Marco dumped Jennifer because he's into you."

Relief flooded my body, and I leaned back against my locker. Then I started to laugh.

"So does this mean I get to be the new Ms. Milo High?"

Violet's brow wrinkled. "I thought you'd be pissed to have another rumor going around."

"Well, yeah, but that one's so dumb, it's kind of funny."

Violet's face smoothed out and she snorted. "Yeah, like Mr. Shallow would ever actually want to date a human being. And like you'd even consider him!"

A thought suddenly occurred to me. "Does this mean the rumors about my dad are finally going to drop?" I asked.

Violet considered. "Well, the breakup is the top story of the day, but of course everyone thinks it was caused by the stuff about your dad. So no, I think it's just going to add fuel to the fire."

I tapped my foot, making a dull clicking sound on the plastic mat covering the locker area. "Why does the breakup have to be about me? Couldn't they come up with another reason?"

"Well, you'd think, but since people are just

finding out about the breakup, my guess is that you'll still be in the middle of it."

The Milo High gossip mill had gotten it partially right for once, but it just figured that it wasn't going to help me. Marco *had* dumped Jennifer because of the rumors about my dad—just not for the reason people guessed. And of course they guessed something that meant more gossip. "Man, it so figures that the next big rumor just sucks me in further."

Violet made a sympathetic clucking noise. "Listen, I have to go, but keep your chin up, Ms. Milo High—you'll be on top of that cheering pyramid before you know it!"

I gagged as Violet walked back toward the magazine office.

• • •

That afternoon when I came home, my dad was in the kitchen getting a glass of juice. I was so shocked to see him out of the bedroom that I stopped in my tracks, my heart suddenly thudding against my ribs.

His hands were steady as he carefully poured the juice into a thick jelly glass. As he turned to put the bottle back in the fridge, he caught sight of me standing in the hall.

"Hi, honey," he said.

"Hi," I said, my voice an octave higher than normal. Just when I needed him to keep ignoring me and stay holed up in his room, he had decided to venture out. And be friendly. Dangerous things swirled in my belly.

"See you later," I called as I ran up the stairs two at a time.

• • •

A few days later, just as I was opening the front door after school, my mom called me into the kitchen, where she was pulling a baking sheet out of the oven. "Hey, sweetie, I made your favorite cookies, lemon poppy seed." I heard the baking pan clatter as she set it on the stove.

The lemony smell of the cookies hit me full force as I walked into the room, reminding me of midnight snacks and picnics with my dolls when I was little. My mom had been baking them my whole life, though it was the first time she'd baked cookies in this house.

She set a plate of cookies on the table and

sat down. I sat down across from her and reached for a cookie, then pulled my hand back—they were too hot.

"So—I was thinking we could get started on planning the menu for the party. Dad's birthday is just around the corner," she said.

"What?"

"The party menu for dad's birthday. Beth helped me send out the invitations last week." She said it like I'd been helping her with party planning the whole time.

"But I thought we weren't doing that!"

"Well, I know my reasons for wanting to do it before were wrong, but the idea itself is a good one. Dad needs the support of his friends now—we all do. And sixty is big. We should celebrate it!" She was looking at me all earnestly, like now I was going to get on board with her or something.

The zesty lemon smell of the cookies was making me nauseous. One good thing that might have come from her new attitude was to not have that party. This was truly unbelievable.

"You really think Dad will like it?"

"He agreed to it," she said. "Here, take a cookie—they're cool enough now."

I shook my head, refusing the cookie she tried to pass me. The thought of eating it now made me feel ill. "I think it's the worst idea for a party ever."

"I can see how it would scare you—"

"I'm not scared, I just think it's a crap idea!"

"You don't need to yell."

"I'm not yelling!" I stood up, my chair scraping on the floor.

My mom closed her eyes and took a deep breath, like I was the one who was being difficult. "Sweetie, sit down and let's talk about this."

"I don't want to talk and I don't want you to have the party." I crossed my arms over my chest.

"Honey, can you tell me why the idea upsets you so much?"

My mom was looking at me expectantly, but I kept my mouth pressed tight and shook my head. I knew there was no way I could find words to explain the things I couldn't even think about.

"It'll be fun—you'll see," my mom said, sounding like she was doing some heroic thing for our family. "Think about who you want to invite, okay?"

Instead of answering, I headed for the stairs. Up in my room I went straight to my stereo for the one thing that could clear my mind: ABBA. I cued up "Mama Mia" and let the pounding beat take me over.

• • •

"I have a new poem in the magazine," Violet said as I sat down at our lunch table.

"Cool—let me see," I said. She slid the magazine over. It opened to the last page, where her poem "Where I'd Rather Be" was printed on the cheap Xerox paper. "This is great," I said, after reading it twice. It was about how lame Prague was and also about all the art museums in Europe that she wanted to visit. "You're really talented."

Violet's face glowed. "Thanks.

"Matisse." It was the smooth voice of Dylan/Cranston.

"Hi." I did my best not to sound friendly,

but he pulled out a chair and sat.

"I just wanted to say that I think your dad is cool, living his own truth like that. I mean, damn, who is the government to tell you what you can and can't take pills for? Reality is harsh and your dad is doing it right." He leaned over and tapped my arm, causing a chill, the bad kind, to wash over me. Then he stood up. "I'll catch you later."

Violet sniffed as he walked off. "Jerk."

"I can't believe I ever liked him."

"We all make bad calls on who to hang out with sometimes," she said, a hint of bitterness in her voice. "But don't worry about it—he *is* cute."

"A guy needs to be more than *that* to be worth my time."

Violet nodded knowingly, clearly thinking I meant good make-out skills. But for a fleeting second I remembered how good it felt to be laughing with Hal.

• • •

That night I'd finished all my homework and couldn't find anything fun on the internet. I was looking through my book collection when my phone rang. I was so eager for something to do, I made the mistake of picking up without checking to see who it was.

"Tiiiiiiiisse! What's up?"

Icy cold slithered through my belly—it was Ceese. "Oh, hi."

"'Oh, hi'? Come on, it's me—how are you?"

"Good." I poked at a blister on my heel, right where the skin got soft.

"Okay, this is so not my Tisse—can you please go get my best friend in the world and put her on the phone, whoever you are?"

I tried for a small laugh but it came out crumpled. "No, things are good. How are you?"

"Well, okay, I'll go first, but you still owe me some truth when I'm done. Things are so great with James, I can't even tell you. Loving an artist man is *always* what it's supposed to be," she said, then laughed. She *would* use Journey's sappiest love song to describe her and James.

I joined in, laughing as best I could. Then she went on to detail all the magic of James and their perfect relationship.

I cradled the phone against my shoulder and began surfing the internet as she blathered away.

"I hear that mouse clicking, Tisse," she said abruptly. "If my life is so boring, why don't you tell me about yours?"

That would be the dictionary definition of boring, but somehow I couldn't confess even that to Ceese. "Sorry, I just have this report for school," I lied. "But it sounds like things are great with James."

"Yeah." The bounce was out of her voice and I felt bad about it. "So how's your dad?"

And then I didn't feel bad. "Fine."

"Tisse, he's sick—he's not fine. This is *me* asking how he is."

"I told you, he's fine." My fingers felt numb and I realized I was gripping the mouse too tightly.

"Why won't you talk to me?" Her frustration radiated through the phone.

"I am talking! What else do you want from me?"

"Okay, forget it. You're obviously pissed at me, and when you decide to tell me why, give me a call." The phone went dead.

I set it down slowly and went to lie on my bed, burying my head under my pillow. God, she was supposed to be my best friend, to know me better than anyone. She of all people should know I couldn't talk about my dad. With Ceese I couldn't hide any of it, not even the stuff I hid from myself.

I thought of how when our cat died, Ceese knew just what I needed: when I wanted to cry, when I couldn't bear to talk, when I needed to pour my guts out. Why was she so off the mark this time?

Chapter Eleven

"So today in chem we were talking about the effects of drugs on the human brain and everyone kept looking at me," I said. Violet and I were in the cafeteria and I was tugging open a plastic container. Last night I'd steamed a bunch of veggies my mom had picked up at the farm down the road. "People here are just so immature."

"Tell me about it." Violet's lip curled like she'd just smelled a moldy banana. "I live for the day I can get the hell out of here."

"Me too." I bit into a sweet chunk of butternut squash. "I feel like they've made me as boring as they are—they're still talking about my dad, so I'm still complaining about it."

"I think boring is one thing you never have to worry about being," Violet said. She was picking at a tray of ravioli in front of her.

"Thanks." I frowned, my mind not fully on our conversation. I hadn't told Violet about the party for my dad. I'd tried to put it out of my mind, but my mom had brought it up again this morning. I wanted to complain to Violet about how much my mom sucked for planning it, but then what if she was offended that I didn't invite her? It could get uncomfortable, and since Violet was the one person I was actually pretty comfortable with, it wasn't worth the risk.

I poked at a potato chunk and sighed.

"What's wrong?" Violet asked.

I was about to come up with something to complain about when she suddenly sucked in her breath and ducked her head. I looked up to see the two girls we'd seen at the pep rally walking by our table. They were too involved in their conversation to even notice us.

I turned back and Violet was eating her ravioli

like nothing had happened.

"Who are those girls?" I asked.

"No one, just some people I used to know."

There was obviously more to it, and I was about to press her for answers, but then it occurred to me that I wasn't the only one of us holding stuff back. We both still had secrets. Since I wasn't ready to tell her about the party, I needed to give her space with whatever her story was.

I was about to ask her what was new at the magazine when Marco jumped up on a table in the middle of the cafeteria.

"Hey, Milo," he shouted. A huge wave of applause made it impossible for him to continue.

"God, he just speaks and these imbeciles cheer," Violet said.

She had a point.

"This Friday we play Mannoit, and I don't have to tell you what that means!" The room erupted in hisses and boos.

"He has to tell me, because I have no clue," I told Violet.

"Archenemy football team," she said.

"So we want all you guys out there cheering for us!" The room went nuts, like he'd promised them money if they'd pop the eardrums of everyone within a fifty-mile radius. And then he looked right at us. "And I know I can count on Violet and Matisse to be in the front row!"

Laughter bubbled up in me, and I pressed my lips together to keep silent.

Violet sank farther down in her seat, a furious scowl on her face. "Jerk!" she whispered.

"Yeah," I agreed quickly, but a wisp of laughter escaped. Marco was growing on me.

Marco jumped off the table, and people continued to stare as he headed to the cafeteria line. I could see whispers and nods as he went. But the gossip around his breakup didn't seem to bother him—his movements were relaxed and he held his head high.

"The rumors don't seem to get to him," I said.

"No, he probably loves all the attention. That and humiliating me," Violet said sulkily. "And there she is, giving us a look, like we asked him to do it."

I looked around and saw what she meant—Jennifer was sitting with her usual crowd of clones and sending us an evil glare.

"That's the last thing we need," Violet said, shifting in her seat.

"I don't know why you're so scared of her," I said, my eyes meeting Jennifer's until she looked away.

"You saw what she can do—that rumor that's making you miserable is vintage Jennifer."

Now rumors were following Jennifer, as people mourned the loss of their perfect school couple. I wondered if she'd heard the stuff about Marco dumping her for me.

"It's hardly making me miserable. It's just a hassle. If that's all she's got, it's pretty weak," I told Violet.

"You thought it was more than just a little hassle when we sat down," Violet said. She stabbed a piece of ravioli so hard, it flew off her plate.

"What's with you?" I asked, more confused than annoyed.

"You like Marco. You thought what he did was funny," she said accusingly.

For a moment I was speechless. She'd heard me laugh. But then I gathered myself. "Is that such a big deal?"

"Yes!" she practically shouted. "I mean"— she lowered her voice—"everyone likes him and no one sees how he's always giving me a hard time. My mom and dad think he's the next Superman and my sister worships him. And now you think he's okay too."

I took a deep breath. "The thing is, I know he's Mr. Milo High and a total pain, but he can be funny."

Violet's scowl deepened. "You sound like my family," she snapped.

"I'll keep my mouth shut about it then."

"Is that a promise?"

"Yes," I said, lifting my hand like I was ready to swear to it. "From now on only negative words will be said about Marco."

Violet gave me her first genuine smile of the afternoon. "As it should be."

•••

On my way up the path to my house after school, I caught my breath and stumbled, nearly tumbling into the grass. My dad was sitting on the porch, his legs stretched out in front of him, a glass of juice on the arm of his chair. He was so relaxed, his head was even tipped back, like he sat out on the porch all the time. Like he hadn't been hiding out in his room for the past few months. Like he was comfortable being out in the open where people might actually talk to him.

I recovered my footing and walked toward the porch, my breath shallow. First he was wandering the house and now he was venturing out. What was going on?

"Hi," he said. His left leg was twitching and his face was flat. But a smile played across his lips as he leaned back, letting the sun shine over him.

"Hi." My voice was soft.

"How was school?" he asked.

"Fine," I said automatically.

"You like your teachers?" he asked.

I didn't understand why he was making

small talk like everything was normal and he hadn't been ignoring me for months. "Um, yeah, I guess."

There was an awkward pause. I could see the trace of a smile left his face.

"I better go in—I've got a lot of homework," I said, opening the door.

I got up to my room as fast as I could.

• • •

The next morning my room was cold when I woke up. Winter was coming. I took a fast shower and ran down to the kitchen to start brewing a pot of coffee. But when I got to the kitchen, I found my mom sitting at the table with a piece of paper and a couple of cookbooks in front of her, and a pot of coffee on the counter.

"Morning," she said.

"Hi," I said, filling a jumbo-size mug with coffee.

"Sweetie, let's do some shopping for Dad's party when you get home from school today—it's just around the corner," she said. "I should have the grocery list set by the time you're home."

I grunted, then took a big gulp of coffee. I wasn't up to this battle so early in the morning.

"I got the last of the RSVP's yesterday. The Davidmans are coming, Josh and Leslie from Dad's gallery, the Rehfisches, and Keith Phillips. Oh, and of course Ceese and her family and—"

I choked on my coffee. "They're coming?"

"Of course! Ceese said she wouldn't miss it."

"I'm going to be late." I dumped the rest of my coffee in the sink and grabbed my jacket.

"We'll talk more about it when you get home," she called as I practically sprinted out of the house.

All our old friends here. Ceese, who was still mad at me, in my house. As I walked, I realized how tight my chest was, how my breath was coming out in puffy whispers. I was tense like my spine had been replaced by a steel rod, tense like my lungs were hard metal plates.

It was time to do something. The question was what. I wasn't going to spill my guts to anyone—telling Violet the basics was the best I could do—and putting words to those feelings was more than I could manage. But at this point not even extended play of ABBA CD's was making me feel better. I knew something had to give or I'd be the first sixteen-year-old in Prague to have a stress-related heart attack.

It was hard to breathe as I walked up the steps to school and made my way down the hall to my locker. My lungs felt like they'd shrunk. I piled my books in my locker, and at the bottom of my bag was the paperback Hal had given me. The mandala on the cover was in shades of red and blue that seemed to glow in the dim hall light. "Center Yourself and Find True Peace" was the subtitle. That sounded dumb, and I almost tossed it to the back of my locker, but then I thought about Hal and how relaxed he always seemed. Maybe there was something to the whole meditation thing. So I tucked the book in with my textbooks for my morning classes.

Over the course of the day I skimmed parts of the book. It was mostly stuff about letting go of desire and freeing yourself, but the goal of meditation was to empty your mind, which sounded extremely appealing. I decided to keep an eye out for Hal to ask him more about it.

I so wanted to empty my mind.

• • •

"Hey, Matisse," Hal called as I headed down the hall after my last class. I looked back and saw him pushing his way out of a locker alcove.

"Hey," I said as he approached.

"So—I hear you and Marco are the latest couple of Milo High," he said playfully.

I rolled my eyes. "Apparently we've been having a wild affair for weeks now."

"Hm, that explains the guy I saw creeping out of your bedroom window last night," he said, his eyes bright.

I laughed.

I was about to ask him about meditating when he waved to someone down the hall. I turned and saw the pixie, who waved at him. She was obviously the perfect girlfriend, who trusted her boyfriend with other girls.

"Talk to you later," Hal said, heading down the hall to meet up with her.

"See you," I said. The book made it sound so easy, I probably didn't need his help anyway.

• • •

Back home after school I locked the door to my room, sat on a pillow on the floor, and crossed my legs. The book said to focus on breathing and, if a thought came into my mind, to imagine it was a balloon and float it away. Then my mind would empty and I would feel clean and alive.

I breathed in and immediately thought of how in art class this guy Richard asked me if I had a drug problem like my dad. I tried to imagine the thought as a balloon floating gently out of my mind, but it was more like a lead balloon, stuck firmly in my head. I remembered how I told Richard he had a problem with bad breath that should concern him more than my private life. This was not helping me feel clean and alive. I shoved Richard out of my mind and breathed in deeply.

Too deeply—I started to cough. When that finally stopped, I realized my foot was falling asleep. I stood up to shake it out. The damn book never said you'd have trouble getting thoughts out of your mind or having body parts fall asleep. I sat down again, resenting the quack who wrote it. Another thought I couldn't float out of my mind. Finally I decided meditation was a scam.

• • •

Friday morning my head felt like it was filled with Styrofoam peanuts. Thoughts of the nightmare party had haunted me—I'd barely slept all week, and I had no idea how to deal with the hellish event that was happening this weekend.

At lunchtime I walked into the cafeteria and headed toward my table. As I wound my way around groups of kids, a path started clearing in front of me. The room, which had been loud, grew hushed. The harsh glow of the fluorescent lights seemed especially bright. I felt people staring at me as I went ahead.

And then suddenly there was Jennifer, surrounded by the usual clone crowd. She stood directly in my path, her arms folded across her chest, her picture-perfect face twisted into a sneer. I could feel a sense of anticipation building in the room, as people waited for some kind of showdown.

"So, Matisse," Jennifer said, her voice silky and pitched to carry across the cafeteria.

I glanced around and saw Hal frowning. At our table Violet was chewing on her lip. My breath felt tight in my chest, but if she was going to go at me for the Marco rumors, I'd give her all I had. I marched up to her and smiled. "What can I do for you?" I asked.

"Well, you can start with your attitude. I'm sick of your bullshit about our team and our school." The clones nodded in agreement.

"Sorry, that's not changing," I said, my voice and smile steady. I waited for her to get to the heart of things.

"Figures. With a deadbeat dad who just lies in bed and gets high all day, you probably hate everything. Maybe I would, too, if my dad needed drugs to deal with me."

"He doesn't do drugs." My heart was beating faster and the smile was suddenly too hard to keep in place.

"Sure, that stack of pill bottles was just in

176

case he gets a headache, right?" Jennifer's voice was cased in sarcasm. "Face it, he's a total loser, just like you."

I looked at her smug face, her big gray eyes and little bow mouth, and felt like killing her. What did she know about debilitating illness? What did she know about losing your dad to an insidious disease that would eventually kill him?

I meant to tell her how awful she was, what a pathetic bunch of losers they all were for saying anything about my sick dad, but words came out of my mouth on their own.

"He has Parkinson's disease. His body is falling apart and he needs the medication to function." I was shaking. Shaking and sweating and blinking back tears.

Jennifer's eyes widened as the sneer slid off her face. The clones melted away, leaving her standing alone.

I felt someone put an arm around my shoulder, steering me toward Violet. "Move," a voice said to Jennifer.

It was Marco.

He guided me to a chair and sat me down in

it. Violet jumped up and hugged me. Hal appeared and patted me on the back.

"Good for you," Marco said.

"Yeah, that really took guts." Hal's voice was like a warm cup of cocoa.

"Seriously, Matisse, you did good." Violet was standing over me, her eyes shining with pride.

I opened my mouth to say that I was fine, that it was no big deal. But at the last minute I said what I really meant.

"Thanks, you guys."

• • •

"So that meditation stuff is crap," I told Hal as we walked home after school. For the rest of the day I'd kept my head down and avoided contact with anyone. But Hal had called to me as I was sprinting out the door, and I had to admit that I was happy to see him.

"How's that?" he asked.

"Clear your mind, let your thoughts out like a balloon . . . who can do that?"

"Well, it takes practice. At first, if you focus on something basic, like counting your breaths or thinking 'inhale, exhale' each time you breathe, it starts to clear your head."

I gave him a skeptical look. "So you sit on the floor on a pillow and think 'inhale, exhale' while your legs fall asleep." I felt a raindrop hit my arm.

"Your legs get practice too; then they don't fall asleep," Hal said. "Give it another try— more than one. It's work, but it's worth it. And I'm guessing you could use some stress relief."

I suddenly felt naked. All day I'd tried to pretend that the entire student body of Milo High didn't know my secret. It was going to be bad, just like last year when everyone kept hounding me about my dad. "Yeah, I guess." I tried to sound flippant, but it came out almost plaintive.

"Obviously you don't want to talk about it," Hal said, picking up his pace as the rain started to fall. "But if you ever do, I'm around."

How was it possible that he was the perfect mix of perceptive and supportive without being pushy?

We broke into a trot as a shot of lightning lit up the sky and the drops fell harder.

"And watch it with the meditation. The book is right when it says it can open you up emotionally."

We were running as we rounded our corner and came up to our houses. "'Bye," I called, dashing up the steps of my house.

Hal waved from his porch and went inside.

I shook myself off and walked in through the front door. After grabbing a snack to eat later, I headed up to my room, stripped off my wet sweater and jeans, and pulled on some old leggings. I took the pillow from my bed, put it in the center of my room, and sat. Immediately visions of Jennifer's smug grin danced in my head. *Inhale,* I thought fiercely, and when thinking it once didn't work, I turned it into a silent chant. *Inhale, inhale, exhale, exhale.* And slowly it began to happen. My mind focused on the air moving in and out of my body, filling me up and then easing out. My breathing deepened and I felt a calm come over me. I rode the calm as long as I could, until the slam of the front door and my mother cursing as she tripped over my bag floated up and distracted me.

But for the rest of the night I felt just slightly better, and a little more myself.

• • •

I woke up on Sunday, the day of the party, with a slippery feeling of dread in my stomach. I'd avoided talking about the party with anyone, including my mom, and I'd done my best to avert my eyes as she cleaned the house and cooked like mad. But now the day had arrived and there was no avoiding what was going to happen.

I tugged on my robe and went down to the kitchen, where my mom was already chopping crudités and prepping dips for the evening's fes-tivities. "Sweetie, want to help me make the hummus?" she asked pleasantly.

"No," I replied, equally pleasantly.

"Matisse," she said, slamming down the knife she was using to cut the vegetables. "Why are you being so hostile? This party is for Dad; he deserves a good time. I don't understand why you're so against it—I really don't."

I turned my back on her, my stomach feeling like it was being squeezed by a wrench. The truth was that I really didn't get it myself. I'd already blathered to the entire student body of Milo that my dad was sick, and Ceese certainly knew about it, as did all our old friends, so it wasn't like some big secret would be revealed tonight. Yet every time I thought of people walking into our home, of my dad with his PD out there for everyone to see, I felt like my mother's carving knife was slicing my insides apart.

"You don't get anything," I snarled. I grabbed my coffee and got out of there as fast as I could.

Back in my room I could hear pots banging loudly. There was no way I was going back down there—I was going to hide out in my room for the rest of the day.

A few hours later I'd clicked through all my favorite internet sites, most of them twice. I picked up *A Tale of Two Cities*, but I couldn't concentrate. I set it down on my desk, feeling trapped at the thought of being stuck in my bedroom all day with nothing to distract me. And then I thought of meditation. I'd done it successfully twice and I really liked how it made me feel. I sat on the pillow, tucked my legs up, and began to focus on my inhales and exhales. At first it was just like the other two times—my mind cleared, and calm flowed through me.

But then I suddenly started having a vivid memory of the day I learned to ride a bike. I was seven and my dad had taken me to Central Park early in the morning on a balmy summer day. He wheeled my new silver bike with tassels on the handles, and I skipped along beside him until we got to the Mall, near the Literary Walk. My dad got me set up on the bike and explained how to push off and balance, and that was when fear boiled up inside me.

"No, Daddy, I don't want to," I wailed.

"Don't worry, sweetie, you can do this," he said, crouching down so he could look right into my eyes. "I'm going to be holding you the whole time."

And just like that the fear was gone. I pushed down on the pedal and took off, my dad holding me steady as he ran along beside me. The wind cooled my face as I raced along, the glorious freedom of speed combined with the absolute security of knowing my dad was holding me up.

By the end of the day he was sitting on a bench, cheering as I zoomed by, his presence giving me total confidence.

It was a small memory, something I hadn't thought of in ages, but having it pop into my head, so clear I could see my dad's eyes shining with pride as he cheered, released something in me, and the next thing I knew, I was bawling.

It had been so long since I'd cried, I'd forgotten how it felt. My body heaved and the sobs tore straight from my gut, loud and out of control. I pressed a pillow to my face to quiet them. It didn't work; nothing worked. The crying had taken over, and I could feel the scar tissue over the wound splitting wide open, freeing all the fear and pain and horror I'd kept locked in me for so long.

I kept seeing my dad as I rode on my bike for the first time, his smile, his eyes, his hand waving as he ran alongside me. Just normal, wonderfully normal. I realized I was calling him, the sound like a razor in my mouth. I wanted him so badly, I felt like my insides were being shredded apart. *That* man, the one who sculpted and came home and made jokes and could run and eat and teach me to ride a bike. Not the shadow who crept around in silence and anger. I wanted my real dad and I was losing him: Every day he slipped away more.

"Matisse!" It was my mom.

I sat up, pressing the pillow into my face and holding my breath. I didn't want her to hear me.

"I'm going into town for some more cream for the dip. I'll be back in a bit."

I heard the door slam and let out my breath. As I wiped my face, I realized I needed to do something. In a few hours a ton of people were coming over to celebrate the life of my dad, who was slowly becoming an invalid. There was no way I could be here for that.

I grabbed my bag, stuffed my wallet and a box of tissues inside, and snuck out the back door, tiptoeing through the house in case my dad was lurking somewhere nearby. I headed off in the opposite direction my mom had gone, away from town, tears sliding slowly down my face. My chest ached and every nerve ending in my body felt raw. I walked and walked, my feet pounding out my anger and sadness and pain.

When the road turned into a dirt driveway, I headed in a different direction, not caring where I went. As the light of day softened into twilight, I found myself near the local movie cineplex. I wiped my face, which felt swollen and sore, and went in. I bought a ticket for a movie I'd never heard of, sat through two hours of car chases and wild gunfire. When that ended, I went to the other theater in the building and watched a romantic comedy. Inane circumstances prevented the couple from being together until the last moments, when music came on and they were wrapped in each other's arms. Movies always ended there; they never showed the reality of life after, like what happened when the leading man got sick and the family crumbled.

It was after midnight by the time I walked back to my house. There were a few cars still in our driveway. I gently opened the front door, crossing my fingers that no one was in the living room. There were glasses and paper plates with food scraps on every surface, and the fondue pot was still on the coffee table, but the room itself was empty. I crept past the kitchen, where I heard my parents talking with the last stragglers, and slipped up the stairs to my room.

Twenty minutes later, when my mom opened my door, I was in bed, under the covers, feigning a deep sleep.

"She's there now?" my mother's friend Beth asked from the hallway.

"Yes." My mother's voice was compressed fury. I heard her take a step into my room.

"Let her sleep. You can talk to her in the morning."

"You mean I can kill her in the morning?"

Beth laughed as my mother closed the door.

I lay in bed, still fighting off the white-hot knowledge that no matter how I tried to avoid it, my dad was sick and he was getting worse with each passing day.

Chapter Twelve

The next morning I woke as the sun was rising and Hal's rooster was crowing. I was as quiet as possible getting ready for school and was out the door before my parents were up.

I arrived at school feeling like I'd been beaten with a bat: Every part of me ached. But underneath that, a new feeling was starting, something I couldn't quite identify. It was like a place inside me had been scrubbed clean.

"Hey, ah, Mathilde, I was really sorry to hear about your dad," said a plump girl with bright red hair, as I dragged myself up the steps in front of the school.

"Um, okay." I looked at her suspiciously as she scurried away.

As I entered the school, I was aware of stares and whispers following in my wake. Just another day at Milo High, where I'd apparently always be fodder for gossip.

I mustered enough energy for a full stride over to my locker and began twisting the lock.

"Matisse, I just want you to know that I think Jennifer is a terrible person to accuse your dad of something when he's so sick." Sherry stood in front of her locker, her arms folded across her chest. The same Sherry who had whispered about me the whole time she thought my dad was an addict.

"Yeah, she's evil incarnate," I said, rifling through my locker.

"Well, yes, I guess you're right." Sherry looked slightly taken aback.

I rolled my eyes as she walked down the hall.

I had just settled into my seat in homeroom when a call came for me to go to Miss Bertram's office. Mr. Lester, my hippie homeroom teacher, wearing a rainbow tie and faded jeans, gave me a sympathetic look. "Take care, Matisse," he said, as though I were headed out across dangerous seas instead of just going to visit our inept school counselor.

"Yeah, I'll do my best," I muttered, stalking out. Like I really needed to deal with the ineptitude of Miss Bertram when I felt this exhausted. That woman would probably keel over if she ever had to confront an actual crisis.

"I'm not talking about my dad," I informed Miss Bertram as soon as I walked into her office. I stood just inside the door, as I was not planning to be there long.

"Oh, well, I just thought it might be nice for us to check in." She blinked as if the lights had suddenly gotten too bright.

"It's been great, but I have class." I was out the door and on my way to first period before she could utter some platitude about my life.

By the time lunch finally came, I was sick to death of sympathy. Everyone was sending me pitying looks and coming to tell me how sorry they were about my dad. As I walked toward the cafeteria, I felt an arm fall across my shoulders.

"Hey, there, pity-party girl."

It was Marco with a totally phony look of concern on his face. I found myself laughing for the first time in more than twenty-four hours.

"Yeah, there's a lot of love coming my way today," I said.

"Well, pariah one day, beloved martyr the next; that's just how it goes." I loved how ironic he sounded. "Hang in there—you can get through it." His arm fell from my shoulders and he began to melt into the crowd.

"You forgot to tell me to keep my chin up and that what doesn't kill me makes me stronger," I called after him.

His laugh, thick as molasses, followed me down the hall. I straightened my lime-and-navy dress and walked into the cafeteria feeling just a bit of bounce in my step.

"You look happy," Violet said.

I pulled out a chair and flopped down. "Not really." I knew better than to tell her about Marco. "I'm the object of much sympathy today."

"Oh, yeah, I bet. All these losers who were

raking you over the coals are now ready to send you fruit baskets."

"I wouldn't be surprised to see a Hallmark card stuffed into my locker before the end of the day," I said darkly.

Violet laughed. Then she gave me a shrewd look. "But it seems like you're holding up okay."

I realized she was right. I was living my worst nightmare. And while the bumbling sympathy was annoying, it wasn't eating away at me the way it had at Friends.

Something had changed after last night.

"I might just be okay," I said slowly.

She smiled. "I never doubted it for a minute."

• • •

On the way home I took the most circuitous route possible, even passing by Satan's goose, but after a good two hours I forced myself up the steps of my house and quietly opened the front door.

"So, you've finally decided to grace us with your presence." The words came flying across the hall before I'd even managed to set foot in the house. My mom's hands were on her hips and her eyes were hard.

"Sorry," I said.

"Sorry indeed! How could you do that? I worried about you the whole night—you completely ruined the party for me! And your dad!" She stepped closer, waving her arms like there weren't even words to describe how I'd ruined things.

I stepped back and the base of my spine hit the front door. "I—"

"You what? Decided to think only of yourself, to let your dad and me down?" She moved even closer, and I tried shimmying to the side, but the doorknob wedged me in place.

"Well—"

"Well, nothing!" She came so close that I could feel her breath on my cheek. "I can't believe you'd be so selfish—I really can't."

"Mom, you're practically on top of me!" She finally moved back a few inches, and I scrambled away from the door and farther into the hall. "I'm sorry, I didn't mean—"

"You didn't mean to scare us to death? Well, you did."

"But—"

"I've heard enough and—"

"But I haven't. Let her finish."

We both turned. My dad was walking in slowly, his wool socks swishing against the floor as he moved. He put his hand on my mom's arm. "Let's hear what she has to say," he said quietly.

My mom took a deep breath, then nodded. They both turned to me.

"So what happened last night, Matisse?" my dad asked. His eyes were kind.

It had been so long since he'd asked me anything real, so long since I'd seen him act like himself, that I couldn't speak. I just shook my head.

"You can tell us when you're ready. Lemon, can I help you with dinner?" He turned and shuffled toward the kitchen. My mom glanced at me with raised eyebrows and then followed him into the kitchen.

I stood in the hall, my breath coming in sharp gasps, tears pricking at my eyes.

• • •

It took a few days, but I knew it was finally time to face what was happening. And that meant facing him.

He was sitting in our tiny backyard reading a magazine, the sun splashed across his hair, making it brighter. I walked up to him, doing my best to quiet my breathing.

"Dad." I hadn't said that word in so long.

"Hi, sweetie," he said, smiling and squinting in the sunlight. His face was stiff but his smile looked almost like it used to.

"Dad, I'm sorry about your party." I felt sweat beading up on my palms.

"Want to sit?" he asked.

I sat down across from him, on the Adirondack chair the last renters had left. Its paint was peeling; and one leg was shorter than the other, so it tilted when I put my weight on it.

"It's been hard," he said simply, looking into my eyes.

"Yeah." My voice was a whisper.

"It's been a long road for me, accepting this, the PD, and what it means for me, for us."

I nodded, not able to speak or look at him.

"I don't do well with weakness, you know? And this disease, it's weakening me, taking things away from me that I love. My mistake was letting it. I let it isolate me from you and your mom, and I let it take away my art." He paused as two blue jays flew directly over us, squawking at each other. "I needed some time to figure out how to handle it. And I think that was tough on you and your mom."

I felt his gaze but I couldn't meet it. I began to pick at a loose piece of paint on the arm of my chair.

He cleared his throat. "I'm sorry for that. But I think I've got a bit of a handle on it all. PD got me down but it's not taking me out. Not yet, anyway."

My hand suddenly became blurred as I stared at it.

"Not for a while. And there's hope—there's always hope that doctors will find a cure, or a way to stop the disease from progressing. There's been a lot of research lately on why proteins malfunction. That could lead to something. And then there's stem cell research."

All I knew about stem cell research was that it was controversial. I hadn't realized that Parkinson's was one of the things it could help cure.

"Right now nothing can stop the PD from progressing, but there's more I can do for the symptoms. I could change meds or have surgery."

"How would that help?"

He absently brushed his fingers across the arm of his chair. "Well, they've found that deep-brain stimulation can help reduce the symptoms. You get a chip in your brain and a pacemaker in your heart, and together they give little zaps of electricity to the brain. Why that helps I couldn't tell you." He smiled. "But it does and I may do that. The point is that there are choices and possibilities."

I was back to picking paint flecks.

"I can't beat off the symptoms forever, though. And I'm trying to find what's good in that."

"How could that be good?" My voice cracked and I regretted speaking.

"Well, it can mean more time to relax with you and Mom. More time *being* instead of *doing*."

He sounded like Hal and his meditation talk.

"I like it here, the slow pace of life, the quiet." He caught my look. "Though it did take some getting used to."

We both grinned.

"And I appreciate what a trouper you've been. You're a city girl."

I let out the deep breath I felt like I'd been holding since we'd moved to Prague. I thought he'd barely noticed me this whole time, but all the while he'd seen me clearly. He'd been with me the whole time.

"Thanks for sticking with me, sweetie." The corners of his mouth twitched up. "And what the hell, maybe I was really meant to be an early retiree, living a life of leisure."

I gathered my courage for what I really wanted to tell him. "Dad, I'm scared."

His eyes darkened with sadness. "Me, too, honey. Me too." He leaned over and hugged me.

I hugged him back as hard as I could.

• • •

The following Wednesday, Violet and I walked to the local diner after school. "This place is a dive, but we'll have some privacy," Violet said as she pulled open the door. "And they have incredible apple pie." We walked across stained linoleum and headed toward a back booth. I sat on the cement-hard cushion and felt something sticky on the floor under my boots. We were the only people there, save for an old man reading the paper over a cup of coffee at the counter.

"That's a great outfit," Violet told me.

I glanced down at my scarlet sweater dress. "Thanks. It's old but I love it."

"I didn't even know you owned anything that was that bright," she said.

For a minute I didn't know what she was talking about. My wardrobe contained just about every color in existence. But then I realized I had worn an awful lot of dark clothes in the past months. "I guess I'm in the mood for some color these days," I said.

The waitress came over, and we both ordered slices of apple pie and I ordered a cup of coffee.

"What I don't get," I told Violet as I handed the waitress the ancient menu, "is how everyone still thinks Jennifer is a minor goddess even though they know she lied about my dad."

"It's the magic of being popular," Violet said, sticking a spoon into her glass of water and pulling out an ice cube. "No matter what you say or what you do, it just slides off. Like permanent stain guard or something." She popped the cube into her mouth.

"It makes me want to puke," I said, and Violet laughed.

"Still, though, you did the right thing confronting her." She crunched the ice between her teeth.

"Hm—that's not what you said after the pep rally."

"Yeah, well, I'm wiser now. She shouldn't be allowed to get away with doing horrible stuff to people." She got a slightly distant look in her eyes. "No one should get away with treating other people like crap."

I raised an eyebrow. "So now that you know my every secret and you've seen me spill my guts in front of everyone, don't you think it's time you told me what the deal is with those two bitchy girls we saw at the pep rally?"

Violet sighed. "You really need to know?"

"*Yes!* Are you kidding?"

The waitress set down our pies and then rushed off before I could remind her about my coffee. I took a small bite—it really was delicious.

Violet wrinkled her nose. "Okay, well, they're Zoe and Caitlin, and the three of us were best friends since fifth grade. We did everything together, told each other everything, the whole deal. But then last spring Jennifer started hanging out with them and making things up about me. Total lies, like that I said Caitlin's acne was gross and that Zoe was built like a linebacker."

I snorted to cover up my laughter, but Violet saw and her forehead wrinkled. "I know it sounds stupid, but it was like Jennifer knew what they felt most insecure about and used it, you know? Caitlin drove herself crazy trying to clear up her skin and Zoe tried every diet invented to lose weight." She poked at the crust of her pie, which sprayed off in tiny flakes.

I nodded, feeling bad I'd laughed. "Yeah, that's the worst, when someone knows your weakness."

"It's Jennifer's specialty."

The waitress finally came with my coffee. I added a drop of cream and then took a sip. "You never confronted them?"

"Not really," Violet said, her tone wistful. "I mean, I tried to get them to hear my side of things. But they wouldn't listen, so I just stopped trying."

"It totally sucks that they believed Jennifer and not you. Anyone with a brain can see how evil she is."

Violet's mouth turned down. "That was what was so hard. I mean, those guys knew everything about me—I thought they were my best friends. And then one day Jennifer sweeps in and tells them a few lies and it was like I was the enemy."

"They were sucky friends."

"So it turned out. I thought my life was over when it happened."

"I know the feeling," I said softly.

Violet reached over and touched my hand. "I sure was glad when you sat down at my table at lunch that day," she said.

"That was a good day for me too," I said. I couldn't even imagine the last few months without Violet.

"Lucky for me Jennifer didn't try to recruit you too," Violet said.

"Can't you just see me as a cheerleader?" I asked, pretending to wave my spoon like a pom-pom.

"Absolutely," Violet deadpanned. "You'd fit right in."

I drained the last sip of coffee from my cup. "But the one thing I don't get is why Jennifer did it. Like, did she want them to be her groupies?"

"No, that's what was weird—as soon as they dropped me, she dropped them."

"So why'd she do it?" I took the last bite of my pie and chewed it slowly.

Violet shrugged. "I think that's just how she likes to spend her time, making people's lives miserable."

"That doesn't make sense. There has to have been some reason she wanted to get you. You must've done something she didn't like."

"Probably just being me," Violet said, mashing some crumbs with her fork. "She hates me."

"Did she always hate you?"

"I'm sure, though she never really acted like it till last spring."

"Weird."

"She's just a bitch."

Violet seemed satisfied with this answer, but I was still curious. It bugged me as we paid for our pie and headed out into the cool evening air.

• • •

"Yeah, so my dad and I are talking again and it's okay. Though last night he was hassling me about not helping around the house enough, so that kind of sucked." I kicked at a small pile of leaves on the sidewalk. The trees were changing color, vibrant gold and bronze glowing in the sun.

"Parents," Hal said. We were walking home from school together. He'd started waiting for me at the bottom of the stairs every day, and I actually looked forward to it. His nutty humor always cracked me up. It was almost too bad he had a girlfriend.

"And the sympathy parade at school is still straggling along." I glanced around as a car sped by and a couple of people shouted hi to Hal, who waved. "People say the dumbest things. Today this girl actually said she could imagine how I felt because her hamster had died of rodent leukemia."

Hal laughed, but then his brow furrowed and his mouth opened, then closed.

I sighed. "Just say it. You know you're going to anyway, even though you know I won't like it."

He grinned, then turned serious. "Well, it's just, see, I think what matters isn't so much what people say. What matters is that they try. Like, yeah, it's not exactly earth-shattering for people to say that they're sorry your dad is sick. But what's cool is that they're thinking of you and are concerned or whatever." Hal side-stepped a puddle.

"But then shouldn't they come up with better things to say?"

"Well, what is there to say, exactly? Like, what would you want them to say that would make you feel better?"

I couldn't think of anything.

"Yeah, no words are going to make it better. But people caring about you, that makes a difference."

We'd reached our houses.

"You are wise beyond your years, Guru Hal," I said.

He laughed. "I'd start my own religion, but all the good ideas are already taken. See you tomorrow." He jogged up the path to his house.

I headed to my front door and walked in. A note on the table told me that my parents were out shopping. I grabbed a banana out of the fruit bowl on the table and settled in a chair.

I couldn't stop thinking about what Hal had said. The thing of it was, he was absolutely right. It wasn't the lame Hallmark sympathy remarks that mattered—it was what lay beneath them. Which meant that Sherry and Miss Bertram, and the idiot girl with the hamster, were giving me something. Something that

Ceese had been trying to give me this whole time.

Something I was just beginning to realize I needed.

Chapter Thirteen

It took about a week to work up my courage, but I finally picked up the phone and called Ceese.

And she didn't pick up. But about two hours later she called back.

"Hi," she said, her voice coated with ice.

"So . . . I'm sorry." My pulse was racing.

"For standing me up at your dad's party? Or for avoiding me since you moved? Or for ditching me last year?"

"Well, yeah."

Silence.

"For all three. And for sucking in general." I

sat down on my meditation pillow, hoping it would radiate some calm into me. "You were really there for me and I just blew you off."

"Uh-huh."

"I just—" My voice caught somewhere in my chest and only a whisper came through. "My dad, the PD—I just couldn't talk about it. It was too hard." I felt tears drip off my lashes. "It still is."

"Oh, Tisse, I know! And I wanted to be there for you so bad, to go through it with you so you wouldn't be alone." She sounded tearful too.

"I know." I gulped, trying to regain control. "But I guess I just had to go through it by myself, to get to a place where I could start to accept it." I felt like I was on *Dr. Phil*. "And now I'm a big touchy-feely mess! I even meditate."

"Are you serious? That's so not Matisse," she said. "Or the Matisse I knew. That's the thing—it's like you were going through all these changes and I felt like I didn't know you. And now you're this new person."

"Well, not completely. But my dad is sick and that changes a lot. Changes me. I don't know; I guess I am different, but not in the ways that matter most." I pulled at a thread coming loose from the pillowcase. "Plus you changed too, with James and everything."

There was a pause. "But I wanted to share all that with you and you weren't interested."

"Well, you can share only so much."

Ceese sighed. "You're right. I wish you weren't, but you are. So now it's all different and you're not even here anymore."

"It's way worse for me. I'm stuck in the middle of nowhere."

"You said things were fine there."

"Then let me set the record straight. This is a town where there's not a single decent restaurant and apple picking is a form of entertainment." It was funny, but as I said the words, I felt a rush of affection for the silly quirks of Prague.

Ceese gasped. "You have to be kidding!"

"There are some cool people here, but some are straight out of a bad Disney movie. Like this cheerleader Jennifer started a rumor about me. . . . Are you sure you want to hear all this?"

"Now I know you're kidding! Start talking, Tisse."

But instead of talking, I began belting out the lyrics to "Don't Stop Believin'," Ceese's favorite Journey song. She shrieked and then joined in. We sang the whole song as loudly and as off-key as possible.

"Man, I've really missed you," Ceese said, after her mother had pounded on her bedroom door to make her stop.

"Yeah, I've missed you too." I felt a little teary again.

"No getting mushy on me, not when there're stories to be told. I want to know everything about your life there."

So I curled up on my bed and gave her the unedited version.

• • •

The next night Violet called while I was selecting my outfit for the following day.

"So guess who was waiting for me after school today?" she asked.

"Who?" I was holding a red sweater and trying to decide if it went better with my superfaded jeans or my oatmeal fifties skirt.

"Marco. He acted like he thought we could hang out or something. I think breaking up with Jennifer has made him lose his mind."

"The whole school is still talking about it." People had gotten over talking about my dad, but I felt kind of bad for Marco. You could still hear talk about the breakup of the perfect couple.

"Yeah, and people are still wondering when you guys are going to hook up."

I snorted.

"I swear, I don't get why he acts like we're friends," she whined.

"Well, you do have that whole childhood connection—naked in the lake and all." I decided on the jeans and tossed them on my desk chair.

Violet groaned. "Don't remind me. You'd think he'd be busy chasing down another Barbie to date."

"Maybe he's gotten wise and wants to date someone more interesting." I stood in front of my shoe rack, trying to decide which boots to wear. Then I realized it had been a long time since Violet had spoken. "Hey, are you still there?"

"Are you saying you want to date him?" she asked in a squeaky voice.

"No, Violet! Come on, no way! You know better."

"Well, you said maybe he was changing his taste."

"I didn't mean to include glamorous city types, I just meant maybe someone more interesting, with a little depth."

"I don't know about that," Violet said huffily.

"Well, then I'm probably wrong," I said. "But let's talk about something that's actually important. What are we doing this weekend?"

• • •

On Saturday morning I headed up the cramped staircase to my mom's studio. Since I was on a roll with apologies, I figured she was next. The smell of oil paints and lavender hit me as I opened the door and stepped inside. I stopped for a second and breathed it in. It smelled like home.

She was so involved with her canvas that she hadn't heard me come in.

"Mom," I said softly, not wanting to startle her.

She jumped a mile anyway, then turned to me, her face animated and alive from painting. "Hi, honey, what's up?"

I scuffed my toe along a crooked floorboard. "I'm sorry about Dad's party and everything."

My mom set down her paintbrush. "I was disappointed, but I guess I understand. You and Dad needed to work things out before you could spend time together. And I think I did push you a little too hard."

"Yeah, I told you like fifty times that I didn't want to go to the party," I said.

"I should've tried harder to listen to you. I was just so sure it was a good idea and that you'd come around."

"That plan really worked for you." I grinned.

"Sure did," she said, rolling her eyes. "But I'm sorry too. And I'm glad to see you and Dad talking again. It's been a hard time for us all, but I think we're pulling through."

I shrugged and she smiled.

"Okay, we don't have to talk about it. But whenever you do feel like talking, I'm here."

"I know," I said.

She turned back to her painting, and I heard the swish of the brush as she swirled it across the canvas.

My steps were light as I left her studio.

• • •

"My sister's making me consider committing homicide." Violet pulled out a chair at our table and threw herself into it. "I cannot be related to her; it's biologically impossible."

"What'd she do?" I took a bite of my apple, and tart sweetness exploded in my mouth. The Prague apples really were amazing.

"Well, so there's this dance at the junior high and she's all excited because three different guys asked her to go. It's all we hear about—how popular she is, how beautiful she is, how much everyone loves her." Violet's voice had venom in it. "And then last night at dinner, she's all, 'Violet, who asked you to your first dance?' totally knowing that no guy has ever asked me to a dance. So my mom is all, 'You're the first of our girls to have a big date.' Doesn't that make you want to throw up?"

"Yeah, it really does." I flicked a crumb off my powder-blue sweater. "What's wrong with your mom? That's no way to act."

"Tell me about it. Moms aren't supposed to rub in what a total loser you are." Violet picked at the crust of her uneaten tuna sandwich.

"The loser is your sister. Come on, who gets asked out in junior high? Just the plastic types. And a dance, so what?"

"Yeah." Violet looked up and gave me a watery smile.

"Wait till you get out of here, Violet. Guys will be banging down your door."

"Promise?"

"Absolutely. They would be now, if you didn't live in Nowhere, USA."

"Well, we do our best here in Nowhere, Matisse," Marco teased, pulling out a chair at our table.

"Oh, do you?" I asked him, doing my best to cover my amusement for Violet's sake.

"Yes, it's a dull life we lead. Peasants leading

peasant lives, graced periodically by persons such as yourself."

I grinned, then stared guiltily at Violet, who had a strange look on her face. Almost like she was holding back a smile.

"But we do try." Marco tipped back his chair. "And we have an event coming up. A big deal for us little people, and maybe even someone from the big city would consider joining in." He turned to Violet. "And maybe you, too."

Violet's face was scrunched like she'd just swallowed vinegar. "I'd rather skydive without a parachute."

"Well, that sounds fun too, but it would put you in the hospital for the hayride, and that would be a shame."

Violet made a gagging noise.

"Yes, it's hard to contain your excitement, isn't it?"

This time I had to laugh.

"Seriously, though, you guys; come." Marco banged the front legs of his chair back on the floor and dropped his joking tone. "It's lame, but it's fun."

"Right," Violet scoffed.

"Going around town sitting on hay in a wagon is fun?" I raised my eyebrows at Marco.

"Well, you just hang out and stuff. There's a bonfire after and everything."

"What, do you get paid for the number of people you can convince to go to this thing?" Violet asked.

Marco stood up abruptly. "Whatever, do what you want." He was stalking off before I could even register what had happened.

"What's with him?" Violet asked, shaking her head.

I sat across from her, knowing two things. One was that I really must be changing, because the hayride sounded fun. And two, I knew *exactly* what was with Marco.

• • •

Sunday morning I was grabbing the paper off my front porch when I heard the door of Hal's house slam. Hard. Moments later Hal appeared, stomping down the sidewalk as though he was trying to pound the cement deeper into the earth.

"Hey," I called, grabbing my jacket and coming out onto the porch.

"Oh, hi, Matisse," he muttered, his voice flat as paper.

"You okay?" I pulled on my jacket as I walked over to him.

"Yeah. I just got into it with my dad." He cast an angry glance back toward the house.

I'd never seen Hal look so upset. "Want to walk?"

"Yeah." He took off and I had to trot to keep up.

"So what's up with your dad?"

"He's a total bastard, and for some reason I keep forgetting that and expecting more of him." Hal kicked viciously at a pebble and it went skittering across the street. "He signed me up for this junior business internship at his company without asking me, because he knew what I'd say, and then acts all surprised when I tell him I don't want to do it, and that I don't have time because of my job on the farm."

"That sucks." I winced as the words came out. Hal offered me profound wisdom when I was upset, and the best I had to offer him was "That sucks."

"It gets worse. So I remind him about my job, about my life dream, and he says it's time to grow up and think about my future. And I tell him that farming is my future and he says it isn't. Then we're yelling at each other and my mom comes in and of course takes his side and in the end they say I have to quit the farm and do the internship."

"Are you kidding me? They can't make you do that." I was outraged.

"They can and they will." Hal exhaled loudly. "They said I had a week to quit at the farm—that I can do it myself, or they'll call and do it for me. And that I'd be grounded if I even considered skipping one of the internship meetings. Oh, and I have to get rid of my chickens."

"Wow, I can't believe that." I wanted to reach out and touch him, but I felt like he was so angry he might push me away.

We'd reached the edge of town. Hal stopped under a tree and scooped up a rotting apple, tossing it back and forth in his hands. Then he turned to the field behind us and threw the apple as far as he could. "I hate him!" he shouted.

"Hate him, hate him, hate him! God, why does he always do this?"

I realized I was trembling at the force of his words, at how honest he was being. I leaned against a tree trunk and tried to look calm. "His thing is giving you a hard time?"

Hal turned and looked into my eyes for the first time. "His thing is forcing me to be like him."

His eyes were shining with intensity, and I was moving toward him, electricity coursing through me. "He can't do that. Not ever." I put my hand on his arm and he leaned into me, resting his head on my shoulder.

"You sure?"

I was overwhelmed by how incredible it felt to have him so close, his weight just right against me. "Yeah, I really am." My voice was shaky but my arms were strong as I reached up and hugged him.

• • •

I was in the middle of meditating when my phone rang. I tried to ignore it, but two minutes later it rang again, completely destroying my concentration. I snatched the phone out of my bag and stabbed the TALK button.

"Thank God, thank God, thank God you picked up!" I could hear Violet shrieking before I even got the phone to my ear.

"What's up?"

"You're not going to believe it. I don't believe it." She was speaking in a whispered screech. "No one can know. I have your word, right?"

"Yes! Tell me."

"I . . . God, I can't even say it." She took a deep breath. "I made out with Marco."

I leaped to my feet, shrieking. "I can't believe it!"

"It's awful, I know," she moaned.

"No, it's *awesome*! I totally knew he liked you!"

"You never said that!"

"Yeah, like you wouldn't have bit my head off if I did." I sat back down on my meditation pillow. "That's why he was always hanging around. He's so into you."

"You think?"

"I know! Come on, you kept blowing him off and he just came back for more." I settled more comfortably on my pillow and leaned back against my bed. "Details, please."

"Well, he was waiting for me after school and I asked him why he kept harassing me and he said there was something he wanted to show me, and—"

"You fell for that?!" I was laughing.

"Oh, is that a line guys use?" She sounded surprised.

"Never mind, just keep going."

"Okay, well, so then we walked to the park in town, over to the playground by the slide, and I said, 'So what, it's just the stupid slide,' and he asked me if I remembered what had happened there." She paused.

"What happened, what happened?"

"Well, so I said no, and he said that when we were four I kissed him under the slide and told him I was going to marry him when I grew up. And then he leaned over and kissed me."

"Violet, that is the most romantic thing I've ever heard!"

She was laughing. "Yeah, it was pretty good, huh?"

"I'll say. It makes up for that lame line earlier. So how does he rate as a kisser?"

Violet sighed happily. "Off the charts."

"Uh-oh, sounds like someone has it bad!"

"I'm sure it was just a one-time thing."

"Want to bet?" I asked.

"No, I mean it."

"I do too," I said.

"Okay. What are the stakes?"

I thought about it for a second. "The hayride."

"What?!"

"If I win, we go on the hayride."

"Now I *know* you think it was a one-time thing, because you'd never go on that."

"We'll see." I had a strong feeling that I'd be experiencing my first hayride in just about two weeks.

• • •

On Monday morning the air was crisp with an icy edge. I rubbed my arms in my fitted trench coat as I hurried up the steps to school, eager to get into the warm building. As I reached the top step, I saw two girls stop dead in their tracks and stare at something behind me. I glanced back to see what was up.

It was Violet and Marco, Milo High's newest couple. All around them people were pointing and staring, but they barely noticed. He was holding her hand, and she was laughing, trying to pull it away. When they reached the path, he bent down and kissed her, then jogged off toward the football field. Violet practically skipped up the path to the stairs.

I stood on the top step beaming, ready to start making hayride plans. But when she got to the stairs, the smile fell from her face. Jennifer blocked Violet's way, her hand attached to her Marco replacement. For a second Violet faltered. She stopped and seemed almost to shrink into her red jacket.

And then it was as though something in her shifted. She pulled herself up and stared right back at Jennifer, as if daring her to say something.

Jennifer stepped back and almost fell

backward off the stairs. The Marco replacement steadied her as Violet calmly strode past them.

I started clapping as she came toward me. She raised her arms in a big victory sign.

"She may have gotten your loser friends, but you took her man," I said, and Violet pumped her fist in the air. "So how does it feel to be the main feature of the Milo High gossip mill?" I asked as we headed into school with everyone staring at Violet.

"You know, I think I like it," she said.

"Well, it's great to be talked about for dating an awesome guy. I guess this makes you Ms. Milo High."

Violet gagged. "No way."

"Seriously, I'm happy for you," I said as we walked down the hall.

"Thanks," she said. "Sorry I gave you such a hard time about liking him."

I rolled my eyes. "Yeah, you're not easy to deal with when you're in total crush denial!"

Violet stuck her tongue out at me. "Well, I really did hate him for a while there."

"Not when you were four and you wanted to

marry him! Hey, I never asked—what did he say to your proposal?"

"Oh, that's the funny part—I actually do remember this. He punched me and split my lip and my mom had to take me home."

I laughed. "I guess he made up for it now."

"Yeah, definitely," she said in a sugar-glazed voice.

I tried to groan, but I was feeling too psyched for Violet.

We walked into school, and standing in front of the principal's office were Hal and the pixie. Her head was tipped back so she could look right at him with her big blue eyes, and he had his hand on her arm. I felt the happiness drain out of me.

"I don't know what he sees in her," I said irritably.

"Who?" Violet was still in her Marco daze.

"Hal and that phony-looking girl who probably wears a padded bra."

Violet looked over. "We may be hicks here in Prague, Matisse, but we're not into incest," she said, amused. "That's Hal's cousin Amy."

And suddenly the happiness was back, blossoming in my chest and spreading all over my body. "Really?"

"Yes, really. And I had gym with her last year—she doesn't wear a padded bra."

Now I was the one with the goofy smile.

• • •

That afternoon I waited for Hal at the steps, students milling around me. He came out of school in his usual overalls and old blue jacket, his hair going in all directions. I hadn't realized till just that moment how totally sexy overalls were.

"How's it going?" I asked, hoping my cheeks weren't turning pink.

"Better," he said, waving to a group of guys before falling in step beside me. "Farmer Dalton called my folks after I quit, and he talked them into letting me work two afternoons a week on the farm."

"Wow, that's awesome!"

"Yeah, I'm psyched about it. And I get to keep my chickens and rooster."

It was a good thing I'd invested in earplugs. Though for Hal I didn't mind.

"But I still have to do the internship at my dad's company, and if I slip up there or my grades fall, I have to give up the farm totally." His foot crunched down on a branch lying on the sidewalk.

"That's a drag."

"I have to do the internship till I go to college." He sighed. "Two years is a long time to do something you hate."

"I can think of a few things that might help you pass the time." My mind raced as I tried to remember the smooth line I'd come up with to ask him to be my date for the hayride. But somehow having him so close made me too flustered to think clearly.

"Funny you should say that," he said. "Word on the street is that you'll be attending your first hayride next Saturday."

"Well, for once the rumor mill got it right," I said, feeling tingles at the warmth in his voice.

"I wondered if you might want to go with me." We'd reached his house and stood out front.

"Yeah, I'd love to," I said breathlessly. He

leaned toward me and brushed my cheek gently with the tips of his fingers.

"Great," he said softly. "I'm looking forward to it."

Chapter Fourteen

When I came down to dinner on Monday night, my parents were already at the table. My mom was serving up penne with mushroom sauce. "How was school today?" she asked as I sat down.

"My English teacher is such a moron," I said. "She gave us this assignment on—"

The loud sound of my dad's plate crashing to the floor interrupted me. I jumped.

"Damn," my dad said. His left arm was shaking and his whole body was waving slightly, as though he was struggling to get his balance. He bent down, and his body slid dangerously close to the edge of his chair.

"Don!" my mom yelled as we both leaped up. "Be careful."

"Dad, I've got it," I said. I crouched down and began picking up the bigger shards of plate, my own hands shaking.

"Matisse, you be careful too. Those are sharp," my mother said, as though I was three. "I'll get the broom and some wet paper towels."

"I don't know how I did that," my dad said, swaying in his chair.

"Don't worry about it; it happens to us all," I said.

"Obviously the meds aren't balanced right now, Blue," my mom said, making me wince.

"I guess you're right." My dad's voice was soft.

My mom swept up the shards and ran a wet paper towel over the area. "Matisse is right, a broken plate is no big deal, but you've been having some problems with the meds lately. I think that's something we should talk to the Genius about."

"Yes, you're right." I could hear in his voice

how much he was trying.

"Matisse, keep telling us about your teacher," my mom said, sitting back down. She was trying too.

"Well, it was about modernism," I began, my voice quavering. If they could do it, I could too.

My dad smiled.

• • •

"The thing is, I don't know if I want to go fancy or shoot for a sexy cowgirl look," I said to Violet, my phone in one hand as I surveyed my overflowing closet.

"Remember, hay is itchy. And it'll be cold," she said.

"Yeah," I said, not particularly worried about that.

"Did I tell you Caitlin and Zoe came up to me after school today?" Violet asked casually.

"No! What did those losers want?" I stepped away from the closet to give her my full attention.

"To be friends again."

"You're kidding!"

"Nope. They know I'm with Marco now, so

they thought maybe they could date football players if we were friends again or something." Violet said.

"'Cause as the new Ms. Milo High you could just appoint them guys," I said.

"Exactly," Violet scoffed.

"That's really pathetic," I said. "What did you tell them?"

"You know, I was just going to blow them off," she said. "But I realized I still feel bad about what they did to me, how they believed Jennifer and never even tried to hear my side of things. So I told them that."

"Wow, good for you!"

"Yeah, it felt pretty good, actually." Violet sounded satisfied with herself. "And that was that."

"And now you have time for the things that really matter, like planning what to wear to the hayride!"

Violet laughed. "I may be the new Ms. Milo High, but I'm still just wearing jeans and sneakers."

I sighed. "My work is never done."

• • •

Every article of clothing I owned was either on my bed or the floor. I'd tried on pretty much everything at least twice, in search of the perfect hayride outfit, but nothing was right. Hal was due in less than ten minutes when there was a knock on the door.

"Hey, honey, I brought you something," my mom said, coming in and shutting the door behind her.

I saw that she had a soft pink bundle in her hand.

"Oh, Mom!"

"I get the feeling this guy is something special, and so I figured why not?" She gently passed me her pink cashmere sweater, the one she'd bought at a vintage store in Paris after she'd sold her first big painting. She wore it only on special occasions, and though I'd begged to borrow it, she'd always said no.

I ran my fingers over the tiny pearls sewn in around the collar and then slipped it over my head. I looked at myself in the mirror, the sweater fitting just right, the powdery pink making my skin glow and my hair shine.

"Are you sure?" I asked her.

"Very." She smiled. "It's been a while since we've hit the stores. How about we plan a trip to the city next weekend to fill out our winter wardrobes?"

"That'd be great."

"Then it's a date," she said. "And you can fill me in on this guy. I want to get caught up on all the juicy stuff." She slipped out the door.

I pulled on a pair of worn-in jeans, then my cowgirl boots. A little lip gloss and I was ready.

I trotted into the living room and threw myself on the sofa to wait for Hal.

"You look lovely," my dad said as he walked in.

"Thanks," I said happily.

"I just hope this young man has honorable intentions."

I laughed, but I also got a little teary. He'd always said that before I went out with guys in the city. I noticed my mom's eyes looking a little extra bright too.

My dad was having another off night, but

lately they hadn't seemed as bad. His pace was turtle slow, but he moved carefully and sat down in the armchair without help.

Two months ago I would have died at the thought of Hal coming over and my dad actually being downstairs to meet him. Now I was excited for it to happen.

The doorbell rang.

"Prince Charming has arrived." It was one of my dad's other lines.

I rushed to the door and opened it.

"Hello." Hal's nose was red and his breath made little dragon puffs in the cold. "You look awesome," he said, making delicious shivers run up and down my body.

"Come on in," I said, stepping back so he could walk into the living room.

My mom held out her hand to shake Hal's, and he moved toward her with a smile.

"Nice to meet you," he said. "And you must be Mr. Osgood." Hal walked over to my dad so that he wouldn't have to get up.

"Don," my dad said. He began to raise his arm slowly to shake hands with Hal. Hal caught my dad's hand in a firm grip.

"It's great to meet you. I've only seen your work in books, but it's wonderful." Hal spoke quickly, and I noticed him tugging at the zipper on his coat.

"Thanks." Though my dad's face was stiff, his voice was warm.

I realized that I was tapping my toes inside my boots. I took a deep breath and tried to relax. "Dad, Hal's interested in organic farming."

My dad nodded his head slowly. "Good for you. That's something really worthwhile."

Hal's fingers let go of the zipper and he smiled.

"I like to garden," my mom said.

Hal nodded. "I noticed you put in some rosebushes. They look great."

My mom lit up, ready to talk dirt and plants.

"We'd better get going," I said, grabbing Hal's arm. If she got started on gardening, we might miss the entire hayride.

"Be careful," my mom said, as though we faced danger in a wagon of hay. I grabbed my black leather coat out of the closet and we were off.

"Your parents are nice," Hal said as we walked toward school, where the wagons were starting out.

"They're pretty okay most of the time."

"They're a lot better than my parents." He reached for my hand as he spoke and our fingers interlaced. My heartbeat was going crazy.

"I think my dad liked you," I told him.

"I hope so. It's intimidating meeting a guy you've actually read about in a textbook."

"What do you mean?" His fingers were toasty, and I rubbed my thumb against his palm.

"We studied his stuff in my art history class last year—I was serious when I said I liked his work."

"Wait a minute, there's an *art history* class at Milo?" I was so surprised I dropped his hand.

"Ah, could it be that the sophisticated Matisse is impressed by a class offered at Milo?"

"I wouldn't use the word *impressed*, but it's kind of neat."

"Yeah, and it's taught by this old retired guy

who used to teach art history at Ithaca College, so he knows his stuff."

I wasn't going to admit it just then, but I *was* impressed. I thought only places like Friends had art history.

I reached for Hal's hand, and after an awkward moment when our knuckles collided, we wove our fingers back together.

All the lights were on in the front of the school and six wagons were lined up, horses hitched to five of them and the last connected awkwardly to a car.

"No one said anything about a wagon being pulled by a car," I said as we walked to join the crowd out front.

"Yeah, that doesn't look so great, inhaling exhaust fumes all night. Let's make sure we don't get stuck in that one. Hey, what do you think is going on over there?"

I turned to look where he was pointing and saw a lone figure holding a sign in front of the first wagon. He was waving his fist and apparently shouting, though we were too far away to hear what he was saying.

"Cranston," I said.

"What? Isn't that Dylan?"

"No, that's Cranston who wishes he was Dylan." I could now make out the sign: *No More Animal Abuse: Stop the Hayride Now*. I looked at the plump horses swishing their tails and shook my head. Poor Cranston really was a rebel without a cause.

"Aren't you friends with him?" Hal asked.

"No, definitely not."

"Hey, guys." We turned to see Marco with his arm around a radiant Violet.

"Violet, are you ready for this?" Hal asked.

Violet wrinkled her nose. "If not for these two clowns," she said, gesturing to me and Marco, "I'd be home where it's warm instead of getting ready to freeze in a pile of dirty hay."

"In other words, she's beside herself," Marco said, wrapping both his arms around Violet and squeezing till she squealed.

"All right, gang, let's get started here." The principal was standing on the steps of the school, trying to get everyone's attention. "In an orderly fashion I want you to start getting in line at the back of a wagon, any wagon."

The rest of what he said was drowned out in the mad rush as everyone tried to avoid the wagon with the car. Lucky for us we had Marco the football jock pushing us up to a wagon with a horse in front of it. He stepped up and then held his hand down to help Violet.

"I think I can manage on my own," Violet said. She put a foot on the crate that served as a step to the wagon and heaved herself up.

Hal followed, stood on the hay for a second, then reached down for me, a question in his eyes.

I was as a much a feminist as the next woman, but I wasn't turning down an opportunity to hold Hal's hand. I reached up and let him tug me up beside him.

"All right, folks, let's move to the front so there's room for everyone." A teacher I didn't know wearing a plaid coat and orange muffler was directing everyone.

The four of us moved to the side, wanting to be as close to the front of the wagon as possible. We sat down awkwardly. The hay, tight in its bales, made for a surprisingly hard seat. I leaned up against the wagon rail, and Hal settled next to me. Violet and Marco sat across from us.

A ruckus at the back of our wagon caught my attention, and I nudged Violet's leg with the toe of my boot. Jennifer and her Marco replacement were being denied access, and Jennifer was not taking it gracefully.

"I'm the head cheerleader—you have to let me on this wagon!" she shrieked.

Muffler Man stood as tall as he could on the uneven bales of hay and held his ground. "It's an issue of safety," he said primly. "This wagon's at full capacity."

Jennifer glanced at those of us who had filled the wagon to its capacity, and her eyes rested on Violet and Marco. Her lips curled like she'd seen a dead skunk. "Come on," she huffed to the replacement. "This wagon sucks anyway."

As they moved away, I saw her eyes dart back to Marco, and for the first time she didn't look like the queen of evil—she looked like a little girl longing for something she loved.

And finally I got why Jennifer had always

hated Violet. And why she'd tried to make Violet's life suck last spring, when she and Marco first got together. She must have sensed how he really felt about Violet.

Violet was looking at Marco with a raised eyebrow. "I can't believe you dated her," she said.

"Call it my lapse-in-sanity period of high school," he said, pulling a piece of hay out of his sock.

I couldn't believe it, but I was actually feeling just the tiniest bit sorry for Jennifer.

The horse clopped at a leisurely pace down Main Street, where a number of people had gathered to watch us pass. Some younger kids and parents waved.

"Big night in Prague," I said, thanking the gods that my parents hadn't realized they could actually cheer us on.

"Yep, we locals do what we can to get excitement around here," Marco said.

"I think we do okay," Hal said, easing an arm around me.

"Yes, you definitely do," I murmured as he

pulled me close. I nestled into his fluffy down coat, which was a lot warmer than my leather jacket. Hal smelled like a clean wool sweater, and I closed my eyes, savoring it.

Our wagon left town and headed down a windy road, the occasional car passing us and honking in greeting.

"Hey," I said. "There's the farm where I almost got killed by a goose."

"Oh, man, I know that goose. She's nasty. She caught some kid last year and pecked the hell out of him," Violet said.

I shuddered.

"I remember that," Marco said. "Good thing she didn't get you."

"Yeah, your goose would've been cooked," Hal said, a wicked grin spreading across his face as we all groaned.

In the distance we could see an orange glow against the tapestry of dark trees and open sky. As we got closer, we saw the flames of the bonfire dancing and sparking. Our wagon veered off the road and headed toward it.

"Thank God," Violet said as our wagon

pulled to a halt. "Both my legs are asleep." She stood and shook them out.

Hal helped me out of the wagon and kept firm hold of my hand as we made our way to the fire. We stood around for a bit, making small talk and drinking hot cider that the student council was passing out. I noticed Marco pull Violet away, into the shadows outside the fire. Then Hal tugged on my hand and led me away.

"Not too far, kids," Muffler Man called.

We slowed our pace until a guy tossing his cider cup into the fire had Muffler Man distracted. Then Hal wrapped his arm around me and I looped my arm around his waist. For the first time in my life I actually understood what it meant to feel weak in the knees. He stopped under a tree and slid both his hands into my hair.

"Matisse," he whispered, and I felt chills dance up my spine.

Then he bent his head and kissed me. His lips were soft and warm and absolutely perfect. My whole body felt tingly and alive.

I felt tingly and alive—alive and very well in Prague, New York.

• • •

After one last kiss Hal hopped off our front porch and headed next door. I watched him for a minute, still feeling his arms around me. Then I opened the front door.

The moment I walked in, I was overpowered by the rich, chocolaty scent of fresh cocoa, so strong I could almost taste it. I heard the mixer begin to whir.

My dad's back was to me as I walked toward the door of the kitchen. He was standing at the counter, steadily and slowly moving the mixer through the cream. The cocoa bubbled softly on the stove.

Before I went in to talk, to joke, to be with my dad, I drank in the sight of him doing his best to keep our old ritual alive.

And then I went over to help him.

Acknowledgments

Without the advice of my wonderful advisor, Sarah Weeks, this story would still be cruising the slush piles. Tor Seidler and David Levithan taught me much about writing and good stories. Siobhan Vivian, Karen Kanarek, Kathryne Alfred, and Lisa Greenwald are the best writing buddies anyone could hope for. And Jill Santopolo, editor extraordinaire, made this book a thousand times better with her spot-on critique. I am indebted to them all.

Many thanks also to Susan Schulman for handling the business side with such grace, Dr. Robert Schell for taking the time to talk with me about Parkinson's disease, and my terrific classmates at the New School: Lara Saguisag, Ebony Wilkins, Mary Ann Yashima, and Faye Mermey. Huge thanks also to Amy Ryan for creating a cover I adore and to Lisa Graff for crucial technical assistance.

Special thanks to my sister, Sam, for unflagging support, and to my mom for excellent mom praise. Also to my super-terrific husband and kids for absolutely everything.

Most all, I am thankful for the time that I had with my dad. I only wish it had been longer.